My God, he wa... enough too!

Dark, slightly wa... Scandinavian sailor's, and a physique that looked to be as well-honed as that of a long distance runner, yet more massive and imposing. Was it all this that her sister had fallen for? It must be, and it made Hannah very angry. Dr Eden Hartfield was the kind of man who would use his good looks to get a naïve young woman where he wanted her. . .

Dear Reader

August is for holidays and the four books this month should beguile your time. Caroline Anderson offers ROLE PLAY, where GP Leo hides his emotions; family difficulties abound in Lilian Darcy's CONFLICTING LOYALTIES alongside an insight to a burns unit; ONGOING CARE by Mary Hawkins continues the theme raised in PRIORITY CARE and updates those people; and, in A DEDICATED VET by Carol Wood, Gina has a lot to prove about herself. All good stuff!

The Editor

!!!STOP PRESS!!! If you enjoy reading these medical books, have you ever thought of writing one? We are always looking for new writers for LOVE ON CALL, and want to hear from you. Send for the guidelines, with SAE, and start writing!

Lilian Darcy is Australian, but on her marriage made her home in America. She writes for theatre, film and television, as well as romantic fiction, and she likes winter sports, music, travel and the study of languages. Hospital volunteer work and friends in the medical profession provide the research background for her novels; she enjoys being able to create realistic modern stories, believable characters, and a romance that will stand the test of time.

Recent titles by the same author:

CONFLICTING LOYALTIES

BY

LILIAN DARCY

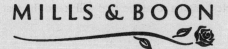

MILLS & BOON LIMITED
ETON HOUSE, 18–24 PARADISE ROAD
RICHMOND, SURREY, TW9 1SR

MILLS & BOON, the Rose Device and LOVE ON CALL are trademarks of the publisher.

First published in Great Britain 1994 by Mills & Boon Limited

© Lilian Darcy 1994

Australian copyright 1994   Philippine copyright 1994 This edition 1994

ISBN 0 263 78732 X

Set in 10 on 11 pt Linotron Times 03-9408-57068

Typeset in Great Britain by Centracet Limited, Cambridge Made and printed in Great Britain

CHAPTER ONE

'THIS your first visit to Canberra?'

'No, actually I lived here for a number of years.'

'You sound English.' Hannah Lombard's fellow passenger on this modest-sized aircraft sounded faintly accusing, but she answered him cheerfully enough.

'I've been living in London for eight years,' she said. 'Everyone there still tells me I sound Australian!'

The older man chuckled, then each sat back in silence for the aeroplane's final descent. Hannah was not sorry that the conversation had come to an end. The long flight from London, via Athens, Bangkok and Sydney, had been a limbo in which fatigue had soon dominated all other feelings, but, now that it was almost over, she had a lot to think about.

Looking out of the window as the aircraft skimmed over low, scrubby hills, Hannah could already see that Canberra had changed in eight years. Australia's modern capital was still growing fast, with suburbs springing up in open, outlying valleys that had once been sheep-farming country. The city centre had expanded, and there was the silvery glint of water where a new artificial lake formed a scenic centrepiece in one of the recently developed valleys.

Canberra's changed. . .and so have I, she thought with a sudden apprehension. Would ghosts from the past meet her around every street corner? Actually, I've probably got more ghosts in London, she realised, thinking of Patrick Lacey and the drawn-out pain of their doomed affair.

Patrick. . . This reminded her, inevitably, of the

reason why she was here: Gina Lombard, her half-
sister and younger than her by ten years, who absolutely *mustn't* be allowed to make the same kind of
mistake.

Galvanised by this thought into shaking off her flight-
induced fatigue and disorientation, Hannah descended
from the plane on to a tarmac buffeted by September
winds and made her way quickly to the terminal
building. Several minutes later her luggage was
unloaded and it was with a rather wry expression that
she bundled it on to a baggage cart and set off in search
of a taxi.

Eight years' worth of possessions from her life in
London sold, given away or otherwise disposed of until
they had been reduced to this: two large suitcases, a
canvas hold-all and a cheap nylon overnight bag to
carry with her on the flight. Taxes and salary, lease and
phone bill — these sorts of things, too, had been paid,
received, discharged and finalised, so that now she had
no practical links left with England at all. Canberra
would be her home once more, for the indefinite
future.

I shouldn't have stayed away for so long, she
thought. I should have come home four years ago when
Alice remarried. Alice, the stepmother with whom she
had had a cordial but not always easy relationship. 'I
should have known that Gina would get into trouble
when Alice and Ray moved to Perth. Why did I just
let it slide?'

Well, that was an easy one. Patrick Lacey again.
Four years ago their long affair had been at its height,
and it hadn't even occurred to her then that everything
he said about leaving his wife, leaving a marriage that
was 'empty and hollow', might be just meaningless
talk. In cynical hindsight, it now seemed incredible to
Hannah that it had taken her two and a half more years

of increasing unhappiness to realise the truth: Patrick was never going to leave Helen, and had never truly intended to.

Four years of her emotional life wasted over it all, and that didn't count the past eighteen months of slow, careful healing following the clean break she had made with the man. Dr Hannah Lombard was thirty-four now. Georgina Lombard, RN, was twenty-four. 'And if I was naïve at twenty-eight when it started with Patrick, she must be far more so with this. . .this *Hartfield* character!'

She hissed the name under her breath then transformed the narrowing of her full, pretty lips into a smile in order not to alarm the taxi driver who had just stowed away the last of her bags in his boot. It had been an unsatisfying sort of hiss, anyway. Gina's effusive and distressing letter four weeks ago had been written in her usual illegible scrawl. 'Hartfield' was definitely the last name. 'And he's a doctor!' Gina had said, but that first name could be anything. Stan? Steve? Even Alan.

'He's going to leave his wife as soon as he's paid off the car loan,' Gina had written, adding, with happy generosity, 'He's going to give her the car and the house, and I don't mind that. *Scribble* and I want to make a fresh start.'

As soon as she had finished reading that ominous letter, Hannah had picked up the phone to dial Australia, heedless of the time difference. Her head had been full of pleas and exhortations which she had wanted to spill out to Gina at once. Never mind about tact. Never mind about the impossibility of conveying anything really important over the phone. 'Don't believe him! You may think that *Scribble* is wonderful now, but——'

But Hannah hadn't managed to reach Gina by phone

at all, not that first day nor in five days more of trying, and so she still didn't know the wretched man's first name. A phone call to Alice in Perth hadn't helped either. Roundabout questions and frustrated probing had elicited the realisation that Alice didn't know about the affair, and Hannah felt that she certainly shouldn't be the one to tell her. On the other hand, Alice *had* heard from Gina by phone two days earlier and she had sounded fine, so this put paid to Hannah's secret fear that there was something seriously wrong.

Even so. . .it became clearer than ever that it was time to go back to Australia. She had been thinking of it ever since making the final break with Patrick eighteen months ago, and two months ago she had applied for a job in Canberra. This last thing faded into insignificance as Hannah made her decision. They must have appointed someone else to the position by this time, she concluded, although she knew that her qualifications were excellent and the three names she had included in her application as referees were top people in their field.

The only thing that mattered to Hannah as she wound everything up in London was that Gina — who still wasn't answering her phone — must be stopped from selling her future to some dishonest philanderer of the same calibre as Patrick Lacey. . .

And so it was quite absent-mindedly that she had opened the Australian-stamped letter in London just two days ago, to read in letter-perfect typing beneath the crest of South Canberra Hospital that she *had* been given the job. An attending specialist in plastic surgery, working largely in the Charles McGowan Burns Unit, which was part of South Canberra's newly established and ultra-up-to-date Regional Trauma Centre.

The taxi descended a hill, curving smoothly along a wide stretch of freeway, and Hannah saw that they would be passing South Canberra Hospital in just a few minutes' time. She was pleased about the job, of course, but it was very much at the back of her mind at the moment. She wasn't due to start for another four weeks, and there was just one thing she was determined to accomplish in that time — Dr Question Mark Hartfield would be sent packing from Gina's life with his tail between his legs.

Ten more minutes in the taxi brought Hannah to the cream brick two-bedroom house that Gina rented in one of Canberra's new outlying suburbs. It looked like a nice enough place, about three years old with a young garden beginning to grow up around it that was very similar to the gardens of all its neighbours. Lawn, a few groupings of shrubs mulched with bark chips, a paved pathway leading to the front steps. . .

Hannah helped the taxi driver to convey her luggage up those steps, paid the man off, then rang the electric doorbell. She could hear it pealing inside the house but no one came, and she wasn't very surprised. The front curtains were drawn, the garden hose was wound into a neat coil.

For a moment she allowed herself to feel a futile disappointment and realised that she had been hoping against hope to find Gina here — miserable and distraught over the end of the affair, perhaps, but *here* — where Hannah could harness a sisterly love that was almost maternal and help the younger woman to pull her life together again.

With her full, dark halo of hair buffed by the breeze and her grey eyes very serious, Hannah looked around her one last time and said aloud with a sigh to the wind, 'So, she's gone with him and I'm too late.' For a moment she wished that she had buried her head in the sand and stayed in London, then she knew that this would have been impossible.

Leaving her luggage on the front porch, she went
through a side gate and around to the back door. Yes,
according to old family custom, there was an empty
flowerpot sitting there upside down. No key beneath
it. Nothing quite so obvious as that for the Lombards.
The flowerpot was a clue, and, several yards away in
an old wheelbarrow containing pots of herbs, Hannah
found the empty pot's twin, picked up and shook the
large shell that sat in it among the thyme as if for
ornamentation, and out fell the keys.

'Excuse me!' A sandy-haired woman in her forties
called loudly across the neighbouring fence at that
moment and Hannah started guiltily, keys in hand.

'I'm not a. . . That is, I'm——'

'Hannah,' nodded the woman. 'She has your picture
on top of the TV.'

'Oh, does she?' Hannah came over to the wooden
fence, cheered by this sudden connection. This was the
kind of old-fashioned neighbour who knew everyone's
business, clearly, and at the moment that was just what
she wanted.

'She's gone away,' the neighbour said. 'She didn't
tell you?'

'No. At least. . . I'm not surprised, though,' Hannah
admitted.

The woman's light brown eyes narrowed in disapproval. 'Queensland,' she said. 'She didn't tell me why,
or who with, but I can guess.'

'Not. . .?'

'Yes. That Dr Hartfield. I don't blame you for being
worried about the whole thing,' the neighbour sym-
pathised with witch-like perception. 'Is it why you've
come?'

'Yes,' Hannah admitted. 'Partly, anyway. . .' Then,
breaking her last vestiges of reserve in the face of this
stranger's almost hypnotic attention, she said, 'I got a

letter from her a few weeks ago telling me about the
. . .the. . .'

'The affair.'

'. . .and I knew I had to come home, but I haven't
been able to contact her. If I didn't know that she's
been ringing my stepmother regularly, I'd be really
worried about her. How long has she been gone, and
when is she due back? Or. . .'

'She went a month ago. My David is doing her
garden for her. We're David and Patty Bolton, by the
way. It's not much trouble to do the lawn when he has
the mower out, and I pop over to water the plants if it
hasn't rained. Four months altogether, she told us. A
temporary job in Queensland.'

'Her or him?'

'She didn't say. But my guess is that it's him and that
she's expecting the four months to turn into forever.
She had a look about her when she came over to leave
me her keys. . .'

'Yes. . .' Hannah stared tiredly at the closed-up
house.

'I could be wrong about the whole thing, of course,'
Mrs Bolton came in helpfully.

'I doubt it. . .'

'You'll be staying in the house, I expect.'

'I was planning to, yes. For a few days, anyway.'

'She turned the power off, and the water-heater.
That's gas. There's a little room off the laundry where
those things are. David will be home at half-past five if
you need help in switching them back on.'

'Oh, I should be able to manage.'

'Yes, you're a doctor, aren't you? So I expect you're
very competent. Straight from London today?'

'Yes.' Hannah smothered a yawn as she spoke, and
didn't feel competent at all.

'Then you'll be exhausted and you won't want to

shop for food today. I'll bring over a few things later on.'

'Oh, please. . .'

The board fence was too high to permit Mrs Bolton to pat Hannah's arm, but the latter got the impression that, if it hadn't been, a very warm, reassuring pat would have been given.

'Gina's a nice girl,' the older woman said. 'And always so merry and cheerful. She gave us a lot of help last year when David fell off the roof and broke his back. I'm only too happy to have a chance to do something in return, and I'm very glad you've come. I've been as worried about her as you are, and there's been a change in her since this Hartfield fellow entered the picture.'

'Then she told you that he's married, and ——'

'She didn't have to tell me. When someone has a boyfriend who never comes on weekends and always leaves by nine at night. . . When she never gets dressed up to go out somewhere special with him, but just mooches around waiting for him to come. . . I soon got the idea.'

'Yes, it's such a tell-tale pattern, isn't it?' Hannah said through a tightened throat.

Mooching around waiting for him to come. . .and then hearing the phone ring and knowing even before she picked it up that it would be him, having to cancel because one of the children was sick at home; his wife was frazzled, and she would be suspicious if he left the house. Dressing up 'special', *not* to go out because that was too risky, but to create a candlelit dinner for two at home that no one else could possibly find out about. That, and a dozen other scenarios, all too familiar to Hannah's memory.

'You found the other keys, I see,' Mrs Bolton was saying.

'Yes.' Hannah managed a laugh. 'And I suppose any burglar worth his salt would find them, too, if he looked.'

'I'll keep the ones she gave me, though, shall I? I haven't needed to go into the house yet, but. . .'

'Yes, do keep them. I don't know how long I'll be staying.'

'Might try to track her down in Queensland?'

Hannah smiled a little helplessly. 'We'll see.'

Two minutes later, she was inside the house, with her luggage cluttering the small hallway. The place was clean, neat and cheerfully, if quite cheaply, furnished but clearly unoccupied. 'I might as well take the main bedroom,' Hannah said aloud.

A restlessness had come over her now and she spent half an hour turning on power, water and heat, unpacking some immediate needs and prowling through the contents of the pantry. Gina must have gone off in a bit of a disorganised daze, as there were still plenty of tins and packets, and, when Mrs Bolton appeared at the front door with a laden basket containing milk, bread, eggs, butter, cheese, fruit and lettuce, Hannah knew she could spend the next three days, if necessary, holed up in the house trying to track down her sister's exact whereabouts.

'I won't stay,' Mrs Bolton said. 'It's almost four and the kids are due home from school any minute.'

'Almost four. . .'

The time didn't seem quite real, and Hannah hadn't yet re-set the electric clocks in kitchen and bedroom. She took the basket gratefully and began to put things in the fridge, which was humming as it cooled after being switched off for a month. Four o'clock on a Tuesday afternoon. Office hours. And What's-his-name Hartfield was a doctor.

With a sudden chill feeling of purpose, Hannah left

the fruit and lettuce on the kitchen counter-top and
went to the telephone on its small table in the lounge.
Canberra's modestly proportioned telephone directory
sat beneath it and she picked up the book and leafed
through it until she found 'H' in the white pages.
Several Hartfields listed. None designated as a doctor,
or with an office address, and since she didn't know the
initial. . . She turned to the Yellow Pages and found
the listing for 'Medical Practitioners'.

Hartfield. Dr E. J. There it was.

For a full minute, she sat staring at the name, not
having expected, for some reason, that it would be so
easy. Still feeling very cold, and with hands that were
quite clammy as she picked up the instrument, Hannah
dialled.

The brisk, automatic greeting of the receptionist at
the other end was not unexpected. 'Eden Hartfield's
office.' Eden. Unusual. No wonder she hadn't been
able to read the name in Gina's letter.

'Could you please tell me how I might get in touch
with Dr Hartfield?' she said, using her best professional
manner, honed now by more than eight years as a
qualified doctor herself.

'Oh, you're in luck, actually.' The receptionist's
voice was bright now. 'He has office hours on Tuesday
afternoons. But. . .how can he help you? Do you want
an appointment, or. . .?'

'You mean he's there now?'

'He certainly is. He's with a patient, though, so. . .'

'He's not in Queensland?'

'No, heavens; that's not until December.'

'Oh, I see. I thought. . .' For a moment Hannah was
quite bewildered and at a loss, then suddenly she was
so utterly furious that the receiver shook in her hand
and she had to clutch at the instrument with knuckles
that had turned white.

What kind of rings was the man running around Gina? If she was in Queensland and he was here until December, three months away, what on earth was going on? With a voice that was still as polite and professional as before but now threaded with pure steel, Hannah said, 'Then I'd like to speak with him, if I may. My name is Dr Hannah Lombard.'

'Dr Lombard? Calling from London? Oh, heavens, why didn't you say so? I'll put you straight through.'

With no time to explain that she was not calling from London, and with only a moment to feel more confused than ever—she had expected that Eden Hartfield would recognise her last name, but not that his receptionist would—Hannah was put through.

'Eden Hartfield,' growled a low, masculine voice that sounded busy and preoccupied. He was with a patient, Hannah remembered. Bad timing. As a doctor herself, she knew that it would be impossible to unleash on him the angry tirade that burned so urgently on her lips.

With a deep, unsteady breath she controlled herself and said as neutrally as she could, 'It's Dr Hannah Lombard here.'

'Dr Lombard? What, from London?'

'No, not from London,' she began with studied patience.

'Then you're here?'

'Yes, and I'd like to see you if I could.' Still neutral, still controlled.

'Well, of course! You've just arrived? Damn! I wish I wasn't so booked up today. If you'd let me know. . .'

'Dr Hartfield——' Now it was distinctly crisp. The man's friendliness in the middle of what was clearly a busy day had disconcerted her more than anything yet. From his manner, he could have been welcoming her as a future sister-in-law. . .and yet it wasn't quite that.

And anyway, if things were openly working out between himself and Gina, where *was* the girl?

'Never mind,' he was saying. 'Look, how about meeting very informally tomorrow for coffee. At eleven, say, after I've finished in surgery. I only have an hour, but. . . Otherwise we'll have to wait until Friday.'

'Coffee at eleven,' she echoed blankly.

'Yes, and not at the hospital, please! I'd much rather get away. There's a shopping plaza just across from. . .'

With no wind left in her sails whatsoever, Hannah found herself listening to the directions he gave, and a whirlwind minute later he had rung off. It took fifteen minutes of restless pacing through the house for Hannah to come up with any kind of theory at all, and then it came to her. The man was certainly cool! He had wanted to disarm her and he had very nearly succeeded. His affair with Gina must be over and he had somehow expected the appearance of an angry relative seeking retribution.

Well, he had been right about the retribution, and she wouldn't be fobbed off! Gina was alone in Queensland hiding a broken heart behind cheery phone calls to Alice, Hannah's stepmother. Just hiding a broken heart? Or hiding an unwanted pregnancy, too? Hannah suddenly wondered. Could Eden Hartfield have gone that far? Was he paying Gina off, paying her to stay away so that no scandal erupted around his name?

'Oh, lord, I can't think about it clearly tonight,' Hannah groaned to herself. Her head was buzzing with fatigue and disorientation now, and the rapid shocks caused by her brief call to Dr Hartfield were taking their toll. Feeling more like an old woman than like a successful plastics specialist in her professional prime, Hannah drowned her anxieties in a long shower, finished unpacking, made a cheesy scrambled egg with toast and salad, then sat down in front of the television until sleepiness overtook her and she crawled into bed.

Thank goodness she had the wit to set the clock-radio alarm, at least. It went off at nine the next morning, dragging her painfully from a deep sleep, and she fumbled to switch it off, jarred by the gabbling voice of the morning radio disc-jockey. Her body seemed to feel that she was asking the impossible — actually to get up out of the bed, shower and dress — and weakly she rolled over, thinking to herself, 'Just five more minutes.'

More like an hour and a half, as it turned out, and it was only the horrible possibility of being late for her confrontation with Eden Hartfield that galvanised her with an almost electric suddenness into springing from the bed. She ordered a taxi then stumbled gratefully into the shower once more. Half an hour to render herself human and get herself to their rendezvous! She had been crazy to forget what jet-lag could do to a morning schedule.

To her relief, she still managed to arrive at the café before him. The place had only just opened, and a quick look inside showed only two elderly women who looked like they were meeting for a regular coffee and chat. Ducking out of the café again, Hannah decided to wait outside. It was an intuitive decision, a realisation that she needed to be on her feet and to see him coming, to assess the man she was dealing with — the man who could very easily ruin her sister's future.

Hannah didn't have long to wait. A sleek and very shiny maroon car soon pulled smoothly into the car park, which was fairly empty still, and a tall, dark man uncurled long legs and stepped out. He waved to Hannah as he walked across to her and she felt an automatic impulse of relief that she had chosen to dress formally for this interview, in a pretty suit of dark red that looked well against her dark, full head of hair and creamy skin.

But she *didn't* return the smile! He was definitely trying to soften and disarm her, she decided, settling her mobile mouth into a tight line, and he wasn't going to succeed!

'Dr Lombard? Sorry I'm late.' Very confident, very relaxed, and he had crossed the distance between them in a remarkably short time with those long strides of his. My God, he was handsome enough, too! No trace of thinning in his dark, slightly wavy hair, eyes as blue as a Scandinavian sailor's, and a physique that looked to be as well-honed as that of a long-distance runner, yet more massive and imposing than any marathon runner could afford to be.

Was it all this that Gina had fallen for? It must be, and it made Hannah very angry. The kind of man who would use his good looks — a type of looks, she decided suddenly, that she had never liked! — to get a naïve young woman where he wanted her. . .

'Where's Gina?' she snapped at him. Why waste time with preamble when all she wanted was to attack . . .and win.

'I beg your pardon?' The disarming smile fell from his face and its well-chiselled planes froze in surprised wariness.

'You heard,' Hannah growled. 'Where's Gina? My sister!'

'Look, there must be a mistake,' he answered crisply, retreating from her as if he suddenly suspected that she was a little mad. 'I thought you were Dr Lombard, but — '

'I *am* Dr Lombard, and if you're Dr Hartfield. . .' Her tone implied the conclusion of the sentence: and I know very well that you are!

'Of course I am. But I don't know anything about your sister. And please have the good grace to tell me why on earth you are so angry!'

'Oh, this is ridiculous! You agreed to meet me here today and I knew you'd have some story prepared about your affair with Gina, but outright denial?' she spluttered helplessly. 'That just won't wash, I'm sorry. I have the letter——' she flourished it '—in which she tells me about you, and now she's gone to Queensland! *With* you, I had assumed. Well, obviously I'm wrong about that, but all the same I know you're involved. Gina isn't the sort of girl who'd just pack up and—— What happened? You've dumped her, I suppose, and gone back to your wife, telling Gina meanwhile that you'll be joining her in Queensland any day. Or paying her off somehow, so that. . . I don't know. But I'm here to tell you that if you think——'

'Hey! That's enough!' It was curt and commanding. His eyes had narrowed into hostility as he listened to her hot outpouring of words and he still appeared to be inwardly questioning her sanity. Hannah glared back at him, silenced but not subdued. 'I'm not prepared for this,' he said.

'Neither am I,' she muttered, but he didn't seem to hear.

'As far as I'm concerned, we're meeting for coffee this morning because in a month's time you'll be starting work as a specialist in plastic surgery at South Canberra Hospital, where I am currently also a specialist in plastic surgery, working largely, as you will be, in trauma care, wound management, and reconstructive surgery as we get the new Charles McGowan Burns Unit up and running. Your agenda for discussion, on the other hand, seems to be straight out of some television soap opera.'

'The Burns Unit?' Hannah gasped. 'The new job? I have that letter with me, too, but it was signed by —— '

'Bruce Reith, yes, our director. I sent you a more detailed follow-up letter a week ago. I take it you didn't get it before you left London?'

'No, I didn't. I didn't know you had anything to do with the trauma centre, or South Canberra Hospital. Gina didn't mention it. She just said you were a doctor. And you obviously didn't realise that I was Gina's sister or I doubt that I'd have been given the job at all!'

Her anger, briefly deflated by this sudden revelation as to Dr Eden Hartfield's professional status, returned in full force. The coincidence was ghastly, but this was Canberra where everybody knew everybody, or at least had mutual friends, and coincidences like this happened. And when it came to choosing between professional and personal loyalties, the latter won hands down.

'Hang on a minute, back up!' he growled. 'You still don't understand. Or *I* don't! I've never met your sister. You're accusing me of something, that's plain. Now will you please tell me exactly what, so we can get to the bottom of this!'

'This is unbelievable,' Hannah muttered, fumbling again in her bag for the by now well-worn letter from Gina. More loudly she declared, 'I don't think you'll be able to re-interpret this paragraph to suit your story, I'm afraid, Dr Hartfield. It's all too clear.'

Snatching the letter roughly from her and frowning over it, he read quickly, pausing several times to decipher a scrawled word. When he got to the crucial part, he swore under his breath, then hissed, 'Steve!' and Hannah was shocked to see the colour and confidence drain from his face in a matter of seconds.

When he had finished reading, he gave the letter

back to her, his hand almost as limp as the tired sheets of paper, and Hannah murmured in some alarm, 'Are you all right, Dr Hartfield?'

'It's Steve,' he answered through numb, pale lips. 'My brother Steve who's having the affair with your sister. My God, I must ring Sally at once and find out what's going on. If he's left her. . .'

'Dr Hartfield?'

'I'm sorry I was so angry with you, Hannah. We've got off to a bad start, but thank God I've found out! Now, I *must* reach Sally. Go inside and get coffee. . . whatever you want. . .while I try her on the car-phone.'

'But. . .'

'Please! My God, if this has been going on for a month or more and Sally hasn't told me. . .!'

He gave Hannah a gentle but insistent push in the direction of the café, then turned on his heel and strode back to his car, almost breaking into a run as if it was torture to go for one more instant without knowing the full truth.

Feeling equally drained, Hannah numbly obeyed his command and entered the café.

CHAPTER TWO

IT WAS nearly half an hour before Eden Hartfield returned from his car, and if Hannah had had any hopes that somehow this whole thing had an easy explanation which didn't involve anyone getting hurt, one look at his face would have dashed such hopes at once. As it happened, though, she hadn't had any hope to begin with. The wrong-footed start with Dr Hartfield was clearly just one more complication in a hideous and painful mess.

Seeing him approach her table, Hannah quickly signalled the waitress and ordered more coffee for herself and him as well. She had drained two cups already, but the buttered raisin toast that came with it remained untouched.

'He *has* left her,' Dr Hartfield said as soon as he sat down. 'This is ghastly! Sally is a complete mess. I don't understand why she didn't ring me. I'd have been able to help in a hundred ways. But she didn't tell me! For some unaccountable reason she thought I'd blame her! Blame Sally! My God, she's the dearest woman in the world!'

'Please!' Hannah came in desperately. 'Fill me in. Your brother has left his wife and gone to Queensland with ——'

'Your sister. Yes. A month ago. A month! God knows how long before I would have found out if you hadn't told me.'

He took a long pull on the black coffee which had just been set in front of him, and Hannah managed a shaky laugh. 'It doesn't look as if we'll be talking much about my work in setting up the Burns Unit this morning.'

'No, it doesn't.'

He sat back abruptly and studied her properly for the first time. Aware of the blue-eyed intensity of his gaze, Hannah was not put off by it. In fact, it was reassuring. At last he was assessing her as a professional colleague and, after the anger and confusion between them this morning, such a scrutiny was a lot more comfortable to endure.

'Another time, though,' she said, 'I'll look forward to that discussion very much.'

'So will I.' They both smiled, a first very tentative reaching out. 'Eat your raisin toast,' he ordered gently, and obediently she took a bite, although the stuff was as appetising as cardboard to her churned-up stomach.

He added milk to his coffee and drained half the cup while Hannah took several mouthfuls of her own, sustained by its richly roasted strength. The moments of silence between them were a relief. The café was still very quiet and the elderly women several tables across had stopped their talk of grandchildren and shopping to covertly study the well-dressed doctors.

Hannah had been blessed—or cursed—with acute hearing, and one woman's words, uttered in a sibilant undertone, drifted across to her quite clearly. 'Those two make a very handsome pair, don't they? Both with such nice dark hair and clear skin.'

'Yes,' came the whispered reply. 'But they don't look too happy this morning. She was here for ages before he arrived. I wonder if they've had a tiff?'

Hannah was seized by an absurd urge to explain loudly to the women that she and Dr Hartfield were not 'a pair' in even the remotest sense—though she had been flattered at the 'handsome' part—but then Eden Hartfield spoke, clearly unaware that he had been the subject of discussion, as the women were behind him.

'So, what are we going to do?'

'Do?' she echoed.

'Yes. Surely you agree that we must do something! Break it up somehow. Sally has a baby due in six months.'

'A *baby*? But I got the impression. . .'

'And the other two——'

'You mean she already has two children?'

'She and Steve have two children,' he corrected firmly. 'You didn't know?'

'All I know is what's in that letter.'

He shook his head and breath hissed from between clenched teeth. 'You must be ready to fry that sister of yours! I certainly am!'

'What do you mean?' Hannah asked ominously.

'It's obvious, isn't it? She's broken up a marriage and a family with no heed at all as to the consequences. Has she spared a thought for Sally or the children? I very much doubt it. But if there are any good graces in her I hope you'll be able to appeal to them and get her to let Steve out of her claws and back to Sally and the children where he belongs. You'll earn my undying gratitude if you do have that sort of influence with her, because——'

'How *dare* you?' Hannah stood up to her full height of five feet nine. 'How dare you assume that this is all Gina's fault? She's twenty-four years old and fairly naïve. Steve is——'

'About your age, I'd say,' he drawled with eyes narrowed as he took the full force of her anger without flinching. 'He's thirty-three.'

'And undoubtedly well-versed in the sort of lies a younger woman will believe about a marriage being empty, a wife who doesn't understand, a mistake made years ago when they were both too young to know any better. Et cetera, et cetera.'

'You sound as if you know all about such lies.'

'I do,' she bit out frankly, not caring what he thought. 'I was a fool to believe those tired old clichés, and Gina's a fool too, and I'm going to make her see it. A fool, but not the cold-hearted bitch you clearly want and believe her to be. You go ahead and look after Sally, slander my sister and leave your precious brother Steve blameless and lily-white in the middle. *I'm* going up to Queensland to see Gina, and I'll contact you when I return so that we can meet to discuss my job. I imagine Dr Reith will want to see me, too, but as you weren't expecting me to arrive in Canberra for several more weeks, I trust my absence in Queensland for a short time won't put you to any inconvenience?'

'No, it won't,' he growled. He had listened warily to this last tirade, but hadn't jumped in with more angry words of his own, as she had been half-expecting him to do. 'Frankly, it'll be a relief, don't you think? For both of us. But I will need to talk to you again before you go, won't I?' This last question was very silky.

'Why?' It was a very suspicious syllable. She pushed back her chair with a loud, careless scrape and picked up her handbag, but he held her back with his next words.

'You don't know their address.'

'I take it Sally does, and you can get it from her?'

'Yes.'

'Then do so, and give it to your receptionist,' she snapped.

'*Our* receptionist, as she will be once you start.'

Hannah ignored this. 'I'll phone her this afternoon to get the information, then book my flight for tomorrow.'

'Good luck.'

'With what? Booking a flight?'

'Dealing with your sister.'

'I'm not planning to "*deal*" with her. I'm planning to talk to her. If there's anyone to be dealt with, it's Steve, and that's your province. I'd suggest that you horse-whip him,' Hannah hissed, and, on that note, she left.

She didn't care that the elderly ladies were staring with open mouths and open fascination, nor that the bill for coffee and raisin toast remained unpaid. Let Dr Hartfield take care of it. It would probably be the only gallantry he ever performed for her.

'Hannah! Oh, Hannah, I'm so glad you've come!'

How vibrantly young, how openly emotional Gina still was, her elder half-sister thought as she received and returned the warm embrace that greeted her late the next morning at Brisbane airport. They hadn't seen each other since Gina's visit to London two years ago, which suddenly seemed like part of another lifetime. . .

She felt rather than heard the sob that shook the twenty-four-year-old nurse's slim shoulders. 'Gina, no! Are you terribly unhappy? Let's go somewhere straight away where we can walk.'

'Unhappy?' Gina pulled back, laughing now. Silvery tears still glistened on her pretty lashes, masking green eyes, but she brushed them away with fluttering hands. 'I'm not unhappy at all. I'm crying because you're here and it's so wonderful and we haven't seen each other for so long. Everything is marvellous. It's so gloriously warm up here after winter in Canberra. Haven't even tried to get a job yet. Steve says there's no hurry. I swim and sunbathe and——'

'But you and Steve. Are things. . .?'

'Blissful!' The offhand effusiveness gave no hint that

there was anything unusual or clandestine about their romance. This might have been first love for both of them, instead of a relationship whose blossoming had broken a marriage.

For the first time, Hannah felt a spurt of Eden Hartfield's anger towards her sister, but she quelled it quickly and stubbornly. If the marriage really was hollow, and she and Steve are happy, why should Gina be thinking of Sally all the time? she told herself.

'Let's get your luggage off the baggage carousel and go home.'

'No need for the baggage carousel. It's all here,' Hannah said, patting her small but bulging overnight bag.

'But. . . You didn't bring much. Don't tell me. . .'

'I'm not staying long. I didn't explain properly over the phone. . .'

'You certainly didn't! I didn't know what to tell Steve.'

'This isn't a holiday trip. I've given up the flat in London, and got a job in Canberra.' Hannah followed Gina in the direction of the car park as she spoke.

'Oh, you haven't!' the younger woman flung back over her shoulder. 'Then that means. . .that man you were seeing two years ago when I was over. . .it didn't work out? You never said anything in your letters. . .'

'No! I never said anything at all, and I barely saw him while you were there. So how did you know there *was* a man?' Hannah said, very taken aback and not particularly pleased. She had planned to use the story of Patrick Lacey as a cautionary tale to Gina, but now was definitely not the moment for that.

'Oh, I guessed there was someone,' her half-sister said. 'And he obviously wasn't making you happy. I heard you crying on the phone one night to him when you thought I was asleep.'

'Right—yes, well, there *was* someone, and no, it didn't work out,' Hannah answered awkwardly. 'But anyway, that's not the point. I decided to come back to Canberra and I've got a very good place helping to set up a new burns unit at South Canberra Hospital.'

'Burns unit? But that's what Steve's brother specialises——'

'I know.'

'You didn't tell him about us?'

'He knows, yes.'

'Then Sally. . .' She broke off and added heatedly, 'That woman! Look at the car we have to drive because of her!'

They had arrived at the vehicle, which did indeed leave much to be desired, and the subject of Eden Hartfield was mercifully dropped for the moment. Gina opened the back of the ancient Holden station wagon, causing a symphony of painful creaking noises to issue from the hinges as she did so.

'Put your bag in here, and let's just hope it doesn't drop straight through some rusted-out patch. Look at this thing! Steve says we should have been paid for driving it away!'

'Surely it didn't have all this garbage in it when you bought it?'

'Oh, that? No. . .' Gina had the grace to look a little ashamed of the old pizza boxes, chocolate-bar wrappers and miscellaneous bits of paper and junk that littered the car. 'It's just that there doesn't seem much point in keeping a rattle-trap like this clean. We bought it from someone's front lawn in Canberra. You know, on of those signs in the front windscreen saying "4 Sale". Goodness knows how long it had been sitting there, and it barely made the drive up here. Steve says Sally must be gloating every time she thinks about what she's reduced us to.'

They had both climbed into the vehicle and the engine gave a piercing whinny followed by an arrhythmical pattern of thunks as Gina coaxed it into life at last after several unsuccessful attempts. Above the noise, Hannah said mildly, 'But I thought from your letter that you were quite happy for Sally to have the house and car.'

'Oh, I was then,' Gina answered easily. 'Naïve, wasn't I?'

'What's happened to change things?'

'She won't leave us alone. She's constantly on the phone to Steve, he says. At work, too, when it doesn't look good for him professionally. It's just a locum position at the moment, in a group practice, but it may turn into something permanent if they like him.'

'Still, there must be a lot for him and Sally to sort out. Married people have legal and practical links which can't simply be wished away,' Hannah said. She knew she was lecturing, but Gina was irritating her — and Steve Hartfield was, too, although she had never met the man. 'Steve says' had already occurred far too frequently in Gina's conversation.

Hoping that she wasn't putting her foot in it, but with a perverse desire to see her young half-sister take this all more seriously, Hannah added, 'You know that Sally is three months pregnant, don't you?'

'Of course I do! Steve says she did it deliberately to try and force him to stay.'

Steve had an explanation for everything, it seemed. '*She* did it?' Hannah muttered. 'It takes two, you know!' But Gina didn't hear.

The drive down to the distant satellite town where he and Gina were living took nearly two hours, and in that time Hannah came to thoroughly loathe the man, and his name. The young nurse was so head-over-heels about him that she didn't seem to have any opinions of her own any more, and whether what she felt was love or mere infatuation made no difference at the moment. Infatuation. . .love. . . Hannah thought about each emotion and realised that, after her experience with Patrick, she was no longer sure of the distinction between them.

At last the drive was over, and Hannah was installed in a small area of enclosed veranda — Queenslanders called it a sleep-out — that served as a spare room in the small flat that Steve and Gina had rented. The place was part of a large old wooden house that had been divided into four, and it had some odd corners and a locked door leading nowhere, but it was sunny and pleasant enough on this warm September day.

The two sisters made a late sandwich lunch then sat on the veranda to talk and the whole afternoon passed away in discussion of 'the situation', as Gina called it.

'You must have had quite a talk with the dreaded Eden,' she accused as they drank tea late in the day, and Hannah was forced to give an account of their meeting the previous morning.

Unfortunately, she edited it so extensively that Gina was suspicious and demanded, 'What's he like, anyway? I've never met him.'

'Oh — er —— He seems nice. I'm looking forward to working with him,' Hannah answered inadequately, remembering his striking good looks, his anger, the distress he had shown. . .and the heated terms on which they had parted.

'Steve says he's a supercilious ogre. He's only three years older than Steve, but Steve has always felt belittled and judged by him. It's really held him back in his whole career, the feeling that —— ' She broke off, listened for a moment, then gave a radiant smile as she heard footsteps coming up the wooden staircase that led to their veranda. 'He's early!'

Her happiness, as she quickly tried to tidy sun-bleached hair, was so open and whole-hearted that for a moment Hannah forgot all her irritation, disapproval and apprehension about the relationship in an over-whelming burst of hope that Gina would stay this happy forever. Then a masculine figure breasted the stairs and Gina flung herself into his arms.

He's not nearly as attractive as I expected, was Hannah's first thought as she discreetly turned away from the couple and drank the last of her tea.

Wasn't he, though? Horrified, she realised that in fact he was very good-looking indeed, only so different from Eden that no one would have guessed they were brothers, and why the elder Dr Hartfield should suddenly have become her gold standard for good looks, she didn't care to question.

A minute later, as introductions were made and greetings exchanged she was able to assess Steve more carefully. Thick hair the colour of sunburnt wheat, shorter than Eden but much broader, as if he had worked at building his body in the gym, a square, pugnacious jaw that hinted at much stubborness but perhaps less strength. . . What he *did* share with Eden, though, were those blue, intelligent eyes. Gina was gazing into them now.

'She's only staying until Sunday. Isn't that disappointing?'

'Till Sunday? Really? Sure you won't stay longer?' But it was perfunctory and Hannah could see that his real feeling was one of relief.

'I can't, I'm afraid,' she answered him, still assessing what she saw. A restlessness in his eyes, a chronic impatience and frustration hinted at by the tucked-in corner of his mouth. Things she hadn't seen in his older brother. . .

'No, I expect you want to get settled before you start at the hospital,' he said. 'Find a house, and so forth.'

'A house? She could take over the lease on mine,' Gina put in excitedly. 'We really didn't decide what to do about that, did we, darling? And I haven't cleared the place out at all. But it's perfect. After all, I won't be going back to it.' She snuggled into Steve's shoulder and he gave her a warm hug, then turned restlessly away.

He *does* care about her, Hannah decided. And yet. . .

The whole thing was such a complicated mess, and she could tell that neither of them had really thought through any of the serious issues. Divorce? Custody of the children? The new baby that was on the way?

'I talked to Eden today,' Steve was saying now. 'He rang. Which is how I knew about your job, Hannah. Congratulations. It's an excellent hospital and an excellent position. The new trauma centre should be exciting. You must have earned some pretty impressive credentials in London.'

'Of course she did,' Gina came in, and once again Eden Hartfield's name slipped by without much comment.

It must have been a very tense conversation, Hannah thought. Eden must have talked to him about Sally, must have expressed some anger, but Steve isn't saying anything about it. In fact, he's not thinking about it; he's just pushed it aside. It's as if he doesn't want to accept the reality of the thing. He's pretending to himself that he and Gina are as free as the wind. He doesn't even want her to settle into a job.

This impression only strengthened as the evening went on. Steve had brought home ripe avocados, lemons and a big parcel of freshly cooked king prawns, and he and Gina disappeared bare-footed into the kitchen to concoct dressings and sauces for them. They refused any offers of help from Hannah, so she sat on the ragged old couch, made cheerful by the batik-print cloth thrown over it, and leafed through a magazine as she half-listened to the giggles and nonsense that proceeded from the kitchen.

'More lemon!'

'*More?*'

'And let's try some ginger in it, too.'

'No, no, I veto that.'

'OK, how about paprika?'

'You'll *ruin* it if you don't stop... .'

When it was ready, they ate picnic-style off the lounge floor, pulling prawns straight from their butcher's-paper parcel, peeling them, tossing the shells into an old ice-cream container and dipping the succulent morsels into the cocktail sauce. The meal ended with fresh mangoes and more laughter as juice ran down their chins.

'Do you like the couch, Hannah?' Gina wanted to know.

'Ten dollars,' Steve came in.

'And the original artwork?' She gestured at some colourful but very amateur water-colours.

'A dollar each at a church bazaar.'

'We had such fun getting it all,' Gina giggled. 'More fun, I think, than if we'd actually had serious money to spend.'

'Possessions are such a bind,' Steve growled.

But Gina added wistfully, 'Some day we'd like *some* really nice things, of course; when we're settled.'

As if this word was a cue, Steve shifted restlessly then sprang to his feet, his broad-shouldered body suddenly tense and impatient. 'I'm still hungry,' he said, already striding towards the door. 'Let's go and get ice-cream.'

* * *

'Dr Reith will be joining us in half an hour,' Eden Hartfield said as he closed the door of his office, effectively shutting out the rest of the world.

'In half an hour? But I thought——' Hannah didn't try to hide her dismay. The fact that the director of the new Charles McGowan Burns Unit would be here this morning was the only thing that had enabled her to look forward to this meeting with equanimity.

'You know perfectly well that we have another matter to discuss, Dr Lombard, and that it doesn't involve Dr Reith,' Eden Hartfield pointed out smoothly. 'In this context, too, I think I should call you Hannah.'

'By all means,' she said thinly.

It was five days since her return from Queensland, and for three of those days she had put off making the phone call to Eden Hartfield that she knew was inevitable. He was right, though. Now she owed him a report on her trip and neither of them needed or wanted the presence of a third party who was not involved.

How to begin, though? She could see he was waiting, and an impatient bark of, 'Well?' came before she had even begun to formulate her narrative.

'What do you want to know?' she managed.

'Did you persuade your sister to come home, or didn't you?'

'I didn't try.'

His blue eyes narrowed and seemed to darken. 'Then it was a completely wasted trip.'

'No, it wasn't.' Suddenly, she was as angry as he was. 'I saw a sister I hadn't seen for two years, and I satisfied myself that she was happy. That was all I intended to do, and I did it.'

Not quite the truth. She had planned to sit Gina down and tell her about Patrick, urge her to reconsider her life with Steve — if not for Sally's sake, then for her own. But somehow the moment had not come, the situation was not as she had expected it to be, and she hadn't, in the end, talked about Patrick or given any warnings and advice at all.

'Your sister is happy,' Eden Hartfield was echoing with heavy sarcasm. 'That's all that matters, is it?'

'To me, yes!' she blazed, meeting the force of his blue-eyed gaze with equal strength. 'It's all that *can* matter. I don't *know* Sally!'

'You only know that she has been left pregnant with the care of two children, no possibility of getting a job and barely enough money from Steve each week to make ends meet.'

'And Steve knows all that even better than I do. Why aren't you angry with him?'

'Oh, I *am* angry with him, believe me!'

'That's not how it seemed the other day.'

He sighed heavily through clenched teeth and it came out a hiss. 'Look, this isn't what I wanted. I was wrong the other day to blame the whole thing on your sister.'

'Big of you to admit it.'

He ignored this. 'Perhaps the whole issue of blame is irrelevant in these affairs. Love is a complex business, after all.'

His tone was very measured and thoughtful now, and she wondered if she was thinking of some experience of his own. She watched the strong yet fine-boned hands that were pressed, with fingers splayed, on the surface of his desk and felt a sudden surge of empathy and understanding. This man was a specialist in her own field and that gave her an instant insight into many of the emotions that must be a regular part of his life.

Anyone who worked in wound care and reconstructive surgery, particularly in the area of burn treatment, saw pain and disfigurement on a daily basis. Doctors, especially, had to learn to cut themselves off to a certain extent. You simply couldn't afford to let yourself feel the pain of each patient too much or it made clear-headed decision-making impossible.

She knew that doctors who worked with trauma patients — seriously injured accident patients of all sorts — had the reputation of being cold and inhuman. And she knew that in her case, at least, it wasn't true. She worked constantly at keeping a balance between clinical judgement and personal understanding, between distance and empathy, so that her patients almost always saw her as an ally not an ogre. She had found ways, too, of protecting herself against the emotional wear and tear of her work. What about Eden Hartfield? Professionally, he was a successful man, but in his personal life. . .?

'*Life* is a complex business,' she told him softly, echoing his own phrase.

He was brisk again now. 'Which doesn't answer the pressing question. What are we going to do about it?'

'Do?'

'Yes! To break this thing up. I said I was happy not to assign blame. I didn't say I was giving the affair my blessing. You couldn't at least persuade your sister to come back to Canberra for a cooling-off period?'

'I doubt it. In any case, I'm not prepared to try.'

'Then — '

'Look, for you this obviously goes much against the grain, but I think we have to do nothing at all.'

'They seem happy?'

'Yes! At least — ' She broke off.

How could she describe to him her sense that, for Steve, anyway, the whole thing had a quality of fantasy and a stubborn refusal to face the complex repercussions of what he had done? She couldn't, and she felt very protective towards Gina. It seemed all too likely that if anything went wrong, she would be the one to get hurt, and any avenging interference from Eden Hartfield only increased that risk. The thing had to work itself out in its own way and in its own time. It wasn't how she had felt in London, but she had realised it now.

Firmly, and not quite truthfully, she told the other plastic surgeon, 'They do seem happy. I think there's a good chance they'll make a go of the relationship.'

'And what about Sally?'

'Sally will find her feet again.'

'That's a callous attitude, isn't it?'

'No. It's realistic, and it accepts the fact that you and I must not meddle.'

'All we can do is stand by to pick up the pieces, wherever they fall?'

'Exactly.'

'And is that your attitude to wound management as well, Dr Lombard?'

'I wouldn't be a very good doctor if it were, would I?' she smiled, taking it as a joke.

'But you feel that you're doing a perfectly competent job as an older sister. . .'

She stood up, hot with anger once again. He had tricked her into making a connection between her attitude as a doctor and her attitude as a woman that just wasn't there.

'Dr Reith will be here soon,' she said, her clear voice icy and very controlled. 'Is there anything you'd like to fill me in on before he arrives? Anything about the trauma centre, I mean.' She stressed this last phrase heavily and an almost imperceptible nod and a shifting in his seat told her that he would accept her cue; the discussion about Steve and Gina was over.

'Not really,' he said. A disarming shrug dissipated

her anger, and she was able to focus with relief on the work she loved. 'We're in a phase of transition at the moment, in which we're still sending our more seriously ill patients to Sydney while we iron out management and protocol problems as we manage less urgent cases. But that will begin to change quite quickly as soon as you come on board. We're borrowing our approach from several sources — mainly similar trauma centres and burn units in Britain and the United States. We'll start to adapt to the particular profile of the local population as soon as we can, though.'

'What exactly do you mean?'

'Well, for example, I've just returned from a year in Detroit, working at an inner-city trauma centre there. I saw some pretty nasty stuff — serious burn injuries as a result of drug-gang wars, that sort of thing. At South Canberra, we'll be drawing on a wide geographical area, as far west as Leeton and Griffith, even Hay. We'll get a lot of cases related to farming accidents, not so many related to work in heavy industry. Some things related to drug or alcohol abuse, no doubt, but far less than I saw in Detroit. Those differences will affect what we do in all sorts of ways, as I am sure you realise. Not only us, but therapists, nursing staff, the social work team as well.'

'What is Dr Reith's immediate background in burn care?' Hannah wanted to know. 'If you've just come from Detroit. . .'

'He was involved in one of the first specialised burn care units to be set up in this country. His position here is only part-time, and will be phased out in a year or two when I'm ready to take over. He's still based in Sydney, where he does a lot of teaching, but he'll be down with us two and sometimes three days a week. He did want me to sound you out about starting earlier than planned. As I said, the process of getting the unit up to full strength is a gradual one and we can take it at our own pace. The quicker the better, though, as far as I'm concerned. We were allowing time for you to make the move from London, but now that you're here. . . Obviously you'll need more time to get settled, but if the week after next——'

'Next week is fine,' she told him firmly and cheerfully. 'I'm quite settled already.'

He was surprised. 'Don't you need to find a place to live?'

'I've found one.'

'One of the town-houses across the freeway? Yes, there are always a couple of vacancies in that complex, and they're very pleasant. Quite a number of hospital people live in them.'

'Not one of those, no.'

'Then. . .' He studied her for a moment and light dawned. 'Oh, of course. You've taken over your sister's place. You really are on the side of the young lovers, aren't you?' he exclaimed bitterly. '"Don't worry about your lease, Gina. Stay in Queensland with Steve. I'll pay the rent from now on."' He mimicked her hybrid accent mercilessly.

'Look,' Hannah hissed. It was incredible how quickly this man could arouse her to anger. 'I don't owe you any explanation but I'm giving you one anyway. You told me to think about Sally. Well, that's just what I've done in taking on Gina's house. I'm now paying several hundred dollars a month in rent that my sister has been paying on an empty place. If your brother has any decency at all—and I think he does have *some*,' she drawled generously, 'then that money will go straight to Sally. I didn't have to do it. I didn't really want to. A town-house, as you suggested, was my plan, and more my style. So don't accuse me of——'

A frown, a rapid shake of his dark head and a

warning hand extended at the end of a powerful arm
silenced her at once. A moment later came a light tap
at the door and then it opened to admit an older man,
a little portly around the middle, with square, metal-
framed glasses.

'Bruce!' Eden Hartfield stood up from behind his
dark oak desk.

'Morning, Eden. And this is Dr Lombard, of course.'

'I'm very pleased to meet you, Dr Reith.'

Her tone betrayed the relief she felt at no longer
being alone with Dr Hartfield, and as they all sat down
again she briefly met her antagonist's gaze. Relief in
those piercing blue eyes as well. It would be good for
both of them to get down to work. After all, it was that
which would be bringing them together in the future,
not the family drama they were both so reluctantly
involved in.

CHAPTER THREE

'How did the interview go?' Eden Hartfield asked Hannah ten days later as they met in the lift on their way up to the Charles McGowan Burns Unit on the seventh floor.

'Well, I think,' she answered him. 'Bruce was excellent, of course, and I think he was pleased with how I handled my end of things.'

It was a Tuesday afternoon, cool and threatening rain, and the unit's director and his new staff member had spent an hour talking to a journalist from Canberra's high-quality daily newspaper. The enthusiastic young man had planned an ambitious two-part article. One part was to deal with the burns unit as part of the new regional trauma centre, and what this would mean about the way accidents were treated in future in the Canberra region. The second part, for which Hannah had provided most of the information, would concern burn awareness and would be valuable in the ongoing campaign to make the public more aware of safety issues.

'I gave him one of those information kits that Bruce brought down from Sydney,' Hannah went on. 'He flipped through it and was quite impressed, I think. If he's a good journalist the article should turn out well.'

'Yes, that kit has been well put together,' Eden agreed. 'We may want to create some publicity material specifically for the local region eventually, though.'

They left the lift together, passed through a small waiting area containing couches and a magazine table and arrived at the door to the unit. It was rather an

41

intimidating door, covered with lettering that warned
about the danger of infection and prohibited unauthor-
ised visitors in no uncertain terms.

Pushing open the door without so much as a glance
at the warnings it gave, Eden went through and held
the heavy thing back for Hannah to enter after him.
There were two more doors now, one for visitors and
the other for staff, and the two doctors opened the
latter and arrived at a row of lockers opposite a large
sink.

Again, the signs above the sink were intimidating,
giving lengthy and detailed instructions about hand-
washing, and again Hannah and Eden no longer saw
them. They had both known how to wash their hands
with sufficient thoroughness for years. Pushing up the
sleeves of her white coat and pressing the automatic
water and soap controls in front of her with her thigh,
Hannah began. She lathered thoroughly, working
between each finger, around and under nails, and well
up her forearms, continuing to scrub and clean for at
least the prescribed thirty seconds. Beside her, using a
second set of taps and soap dispenser, Eden Hartfield
did the same.

And this was where the routine differed from the
thousands of others that had gone before it. Hannah
had been noticing the phenomenon for several days
now, and she didn't like it one bit. Today was. . .she
counted. . .her seventh day at South Canberra
Hospital. She had started full-time a week ago, feeling
nervous, tense and angry every time she encountered
Dr Hartfield — which was constantly, of course — her
muscles steeled stiffly in preparation for a
confrontation.

But nothing of the kind had happened. He didn't
mention Sally, Steve or Gina that first day, nor the
second, nor the third, and Hannah realised finally that

he had made a very firm decision not to do so. He
didn't have to tell her this in words. There was so much
else to discuss, his busy manner seemed to say. The
subject of Steve and Gina was irrelevant, off-limits,
inappropriate.

And so by Wednesday she had begun to relax with
him. Very fortunate, actually. They were together
during meetings, rounds, office hours. . . In future
they would even meet during surgery from time to time
as they had both been given a regular slot in Theatre
on Wednesday mornings. He operated on Fridays as
well, and when Hannah's own case-load increased, her
surgery hours would expand to include a session on
Thursdays — one time in the week when she could
count fairly strongly on *not* seeing him. Once you
included phone calls and conference sessions about
particular cases and emergency surgery in which both
of them would be operating together. . .

I'd better get on well with him, at least professionally, or this job will be impossible!

Perhaps it was this realisation that had made her so
aware of him during their hand-washing ritual. The
noise of water rushing into stainless steel sinks made
conversation difficult, so they were usually silent at
these times, and this left most of her mind free to think
about the man at her side.

She had noticed his hands before, that day in his
office when they had been splayed on his desk with
such force and tension. Now, as he washed them, they
seemed more sensuous — strong, but with an incredible
capacity for gentleness, too. It wasn't just an
impression, either, it was the literal truth. As well as
all his expertise in burn-shock treatment, wound management and the techniques of skin grafting, Eden
Hartfield's speciality was in reconstructive surgery of

the hand, a field which required incredible dexterity, sensitivity, and fine motor control.

Hannah rinsed her hands and arms, nudged the control with her thigh once again to turn off the water and reached for a paper towel from the dispenser mounted on the wall above. If she had been paying more attention, she would have seen that Eden was about to do the same. Their shoulders bumped, imprinting an instant sense-memory of pressure and warmth; they each apologised incoherently and pulled away, neither succeeding in getting a towel at all.

'You first,' he murmured.

Obediently, she reached up to the dispenser again, and was very relieved when he began to talk about the injured child they had come to see.

'We don't know much about this new patient yet. He was admitted through Casualty then sent straight up here. The mother was with him, and Alison should have got together a good history by now.' The latter was a resident, on a three-month rotation through the burns unit, and so far Hannah had found the younger woman competent and likeable.

The two senior doctors entered the unit together and were spotted immediately by the staff nurse in charge of this shift, who said, 'Bed 702. I knew you were on your way up, so I asked the mother to wait outside. Did you see her as you came through?'

'No, we didn't,' Eden answered.

'She must have been in the bathroom. She was pretty upset.'

'Let's take a look, then, and have her back in as soon as we can for a talk.'

The Charles McGowan Burns Unit was not large. Ten patients would be a full complement, and it might be months more before all of these ten beds were filled. Three of the rooms, which opened off a central rectangle of service facilities including hydrotherapy baths, contained two beds, and the remaining four rooms were private. It was into the first of these that three-year-old Sean Carroll had been settled.

He was already connected to an intravenous drip, which was set to flow at a rapid rate, as fluid replacement was one of the critical features of early burn management. He lay inert, now, his pain awareness mercifully dimmed by medication as two nurses worked on dressing the angry-looking scald burns that covered his chest and abdomen, the front of his thighs, calves and feet, and a small part of his face.

Alison Steadwood stood up as the two more senior doctors entered. 'I'm calculating the percentage of the burn area using the Lund Browder Chart,' she said. 'The ambulance people used the Rule of Nines and estimated thirty-eight per cent, but I think that was a bit high. I'm saying thirty-two per cent. Some of it is superficial, but most is partial thickness.'

'Not good,' said Eden.

'No. . .' Hannah murmured in agreement. She had seen far worse, of course, and in children younger than this, but each new patient was a tragic compendium of 'if onlys'. 'What's the story, then, Alison?' she asked.

'Sean has been very keen on having showers lately, apparently, instead of baths. He thinks it's "a big boy thing to do", Mrs Carroll said. He had wanted one straight after his nap but she had said no, and thought that was the end of it. She was getting a roast in the oven, thought he was in the play-room, and was just thinking that things seemed a bit quiet when she heard him screaming. He had undressed himself — left his nappy and plastic pants on, fortunately, so all of that area was protected.'

'One reason to be thankful for delayed toilet training,' Hannah came in.

'Then he got into the tub.'

'Is that the kind where the shower nozzle is positioned over the bath?' Eden asked.

'Yes, apparently. He managed to turn the hot tap on full force, and, since the water-heater is just through the wall, the really hot stuff only took a second or two to come through the pipes.'

'They had the heat setting up high?'

'Yes. The husband likes it that way because he makes bentwood furniture as a hobby, or something. He needs to soak the wood in scalding water. She explained it, but I can't remember the details. Not relevant, I suppose, except that I sensed some anger about it.'

'Not surprised.'

'Only today I was telling that journalist that children can get full-thickness burns in three seconds from water heated to a hundred and forty degrees Fahrenheit,' Hannah said. 'Home water-heaters are easily capable of heating to that temperature and beyond. I hope he mentions those figures in the article.'

'Anyway, Mrs Carroll rushed in and found Sean pressed back against the far end of the tub, too terrified and shocked to climb out. At that distance the arc of water was only reaching his feet.'

'Did she do anything?'

'First-aid? Yes; she did very well. Pulled him out, pulled off his nappy in case hot water was soaking through it, ran tepid water over him for several minutes then saw how serious it was, wrapped him in a clean dry towel and called the ambulance. She seems intelligent and sensible.'

'Good. You wouldn't believe how many people still rush to put butter or petroleum jelly on a burn, and how *few* people think to remove clothing that might still be hot enough to carry a burn to the skin.'

'I'm *starting* to believe it, working on this rotation.' Alison smiled grimly. 'She's distraught now, of course.'

'Hmm. . .' Eden Hartfield donned a clean gown, cap, mask and gloves, and began to examine the boy's feet, while Hannah, similarly clad, looked at the chest and face injuries.

'These facial burns are really only splashes,' she said after a minute. 'Superficial. They'll heal easily on their own. Even the upper chest. . .'

'Yes,' Eden agreed. 'It gets worse lower down. Related to the density of the water flow and how long it took him to get out of the way. I'd say the feet and thighs will need some debriding and grafting.'

'Swelling around the lower chest area could create respiratory problems,' Hannah suggested.

'Something to watch out for,' answered Eden. 'But the fact that it's only the front of the chest and doesn't fully encircle the body. . .'

'Yes, that's good.'

They spent another ten minutes with the injured child, hearing more from Alison Steadwood about the child's past medical history and calculating a programme of fluid treatment, pain management and nutrition for the critical twenty-four hours that followed. All three were vital areas, as was infection control.

Wound cultures would be taken regularly and the samples sent off to the lab for analysis, so that antibiotics could be used to kill harmful bacteria if they were found. The child would need large quantities of fluid to replace what was lost through the raw skin, but even with this fluid there was a danger of temporary kidney problems developing if not enough liquid reached them. This room and its twin on the other side of the nurses' station were both equipped for kidney dialysis if it became necessary.

Pain, ironically, was a good sign in burn injuries, but it could be excruciating, and cancer care was probably the only field in which medication was more heavily prescribed. The healing body needed far higher calorie levels than normal, too, particularly in the form of protein, and, if the patient was too ill to eat normally, a liquid—looking rather like milk—that contained a complete balance of nutritional requirements was fed intravenously.

Finally, they were ready to call Helen Carroll in. She was still visibly upset and in shock, with reddened eyes and shaking legs. Hannah noticed the latter and said to the cheerfully plump Sister Evans, who would be nursing the boy on a one-to-one basis until eleven tonight, 'Could we have some tea for Mrs Carroll? And something to eat? A sweet biscuit, or whatever you've got.'

'Coming up,' Nancy Evans said.

'Will he be all right?' was the mother's first question. 'He's looking worse and worse.'

'That's normal,' Eden assured her. 'The oedema—swelling—is the body's natural response. This phase is called burn shock, and, yes, it is alarming to see. Your quick thinking on the scene has minimised the damage, though, and children are remarkably resilient once this initial phase is over.'

'He barely seems to know me. . .'

'He's very groggy from the pain-killers we've given him, and his whole system is in shock. Just sit quietly with him. His awareness of you will do him good.'

Sister Evans came in with the tea and two chocolate biscuits at that moment, and Mrs Carroll was coaxed into a chair at the boy's bedside. Hannah and Eden left the new patient, knowing that there was more for the mother to get used to later on. Skin grafts, for example. Their decision about whether or not to graft would be made over the next two or three days as it became clear how each area of skin was healing.

There were three more patients to see this afternoon.

'A little earlier than our normal round, but since we're here. . .' said Eden.

First they saw Glenn Hayes, a young man who had received some relatively minor chemical burns to his hands and arms while working on a tractor battery out on his farm in the Riverina district. His left hand and forearm had needed some grafting, but, with plenty of donor sites to choose from, the grafts had been strong and healthy and had taken well.

'There's some contracture developing around the thumb joints,' Eden said in an aside to Hannah. 'But I won't deal with that now. We'll keep splinting it and he can come down to us again in a month or two when it will be clearer how that scar tissue is going to build.'

Next came an older child, Chris Gardener, whose right leg and foot had been burnt when he was playing with fireworks. An explosive concoction of his own had failed to ignite; he had tried to kick it out of the way, and it had gone off. The burns were serious ones, reaching full thickness in some spots, but because, again, they covered only a relatively small area of his body, his life had not been in danger. He was in now for follow-up surgery to restore as much function as possible to the injured foot, and Eden was confident that the operation would be successful.

The last patient in the unit, also in a private room, was one whom Hannah did not look forward to seeing. Janice Peters, aged fifty-one, had received deep partial-thickness burns to large areas of her hands, arms, chest, neck and face several months ago. Her initial treatment had been given at the burns unit in Sydney where Dr Reith was a consultant — she had been flown there immediately after the accident — but now she was

back in Canberra to receive several cosmetic and
reconstructive operations on face and hands.

'Hi, guys!' she said to the two doctors as they
entered, in a voice made hoarse and rough from years
of heavy smoking, and distorted by the scarring which
pulled one corner of her mouth dramatically down-
wards. 'You're early! I didn't have a chance to get
pretty for you.'

She laughed forcedly at her joke. She *wasn't* pretty
with that facial scarring, and all three of them knew it.
There was much that Hannah would be able to do with
plastic surgery techniques, but some scarring, fading
with time, would always remain. Unfortunately Janice
had not accepted this yet at all.

'Look!' she said to the two doctors immediately.
'I've found it! This is the face I want!' She held a
magazine out to them and pointed at the full-page
picture of an impossibly gorgeous, frighteningly flaw-
less model's face. 'Harry won't be able to resist me
then, will he? He'll come back to me *for sure*.'

Mrs Peters blamed the accident and her disfigurement for the end of her marriage. The subject had
come up each time Hannah saw her, and she hadn't
known how to handle it. On previous rounds, the issue
had slipped by, giving way to technical discussion about
the hand injuries or a mini teaching session with the
two medical students who were currently on a plastic
surgery rotation at the hospital, but today things were
quieter and Hannah found herself looking instinctively
to Eden for guidance.

He picked up her cue with a barely perceptible nod
of acknowledgement and she expected to hear something soothing and reassuring from him as he bent over
the woman and stared her full in the eyes.

'Look,' he said very firmly. 'Take it one step at a
time. That's what Dr Lombard and I are doing. Last

week we dealt with the contractures on your left hand and on the side of your neck. Tomorrow we'll tackle your right hand and that pulling on your mouth. You'll be able to use your hands properly again, and you'll be able to talk without slurring. Is that important to you?'

'Of course it is!'

'Then, meanwhile, stop wishing for miracles from us and start thinking about the miracle you can do for yourself.'

'What do you mean?' Her head turned suspiciously to one side, showing the white dressing on her neck.

'You know what I mean. Anne Gallagher was in here talking to you about it this morning.'

'I do *not* have a drinking problem!' Janice Peters hissed suddenly, turning away from them and slouching down in the bed until she was just a humped shape.

Hannah and Eden waited for a few moments but there was no further movement or sound, and she did not respond when they tried to talk to her. They moved reluctantly away from the bedside and into the corridor.

'A drinking problem?' Hannah queried.

'Yes. Our social worker here, Anne Gallagher——'

'Yes, I've met her twice now, but only briefly.'

'She's very good. We knew from the people in Sydney that alcohol was a factor.'

'In the accident itself.' Hannah nodded. 'I noticed that written up in her chart, although she denies it, apparently.'

'She denies it, but she was definitely well under the influence when she fell asleep on the couch with that lighted cigarette in her hand. But the Sydney social-work department doesn't seem to have pursued the issue much further than that. Bruce says they're short-staffed at the moment. Anne has talked more exten-sively to Janice's husband and daughters, who all say

that the marriage was on the rocks well before the
accident, and that Janice is just using the issue of
disfigurement to hide from the truth.'

'Is there any chance that Harry Peters will come
back to her?'

'It's unlikely, Anne thinks. There's another woman
in the picture now.'

Their eyes met briefly, and Hannah knew that he
was thinking of Steve and Sally. . .and Gina. She said
quickly, 'Then it's hard to see what we can do.'

'For Janice herself? Very little. We're her surgeons,
not her counsellors. Anne will do what she can. Meanwhile, I can only caution you not to make any rosy
promises at all about your end of the surgery. You'll
have to be blunt, as I was just now, but we can't afford
to have her fantasising about getting a model's face.
Unrealistic expectations like that can do everything
from slowing a patient's recovery to creating a lawsuit.'

'You're right. I've encountered that sort of thing
before, and I'll be careful.'

They walked past the hydrotherapy room and back
to the nurses' station.

'I'll be back before main rounds tomorrow to check
on Sean,' Eden told the nurse running today's shift,
Joan Harkins. 'Is Dr Steadwood on call tonight?' He
looked behind the older nurse to a white-board on the
wall where staff rostered on were marked down in
green felt-tip pen. 'Ah, yes; I see she is. Good. But if
anything develops that she can't handle, don't hesitate
to page me at once.'

'Of course, Doctor.'

It was Eden who had officially taken on Sean's case,
although Hannah would be involved in consultations
and decision-making as well. Bruce, too, would join
them early tomorrow morning for one of the biggest
rounds of the week in which nurses and therapists

joined doctors and medical students in discussing each patient's case.

Eden and Hannah were ready to leave the unit at last. 'Took longer than I thought in there,' he commented as they emerged into the cooler air of the seventh-floor foyer. A burns unit was always kept very warm, as burn injuries affected the body's ability to hold heat and regulate temperature.

'Yes, almost time for visiting hour,' Hannah observed.

'Is it? Then let's make our escape. Our fire-cracker boy's mother can be very persistent. Asks the same questions over and over and doesn't listen to the answers. I know it's a symptom of her anxiety, but, on the occasions when I've given in to it, I've been stuck with her for half an hour, and then she barely gets in to see Chris himself before visiting hour is over.'

'That's her coming out of the lift now, isn't it?' Hannah murmured covertly.

'Oh, God, yes! I'm sunk!'

'No, look. Here's another lift and it's going down.'

They entered quickly and Eden reached across without ceremony in front of Hannah to press the 'Door Close' button. His arm brushed the open lapels of her white coat, sensitising the skin of her throat and breasts even beneath the red silk blouse she wore. But the arm dropped again, the door closed safely between them and Mrs Gardener, and his words distracted her.

'I don't like to make myself unavailable to a patient's family.'

'No, but. . .'

'You were a willing conspirator, I noticed. Does that mean——?'

'Yes, I witnessed her buttonholing poor Alison last Friday. You're right. She badgers, doesn't listen, and it doesn't do her or Chris any good at all.'

'Even the lift controls seem to agree with our assessment. I've never known one to just appear like that without us so much as pushing a button!'

Hannah laughed and each of them began to shake off the weariness of a long day as they descended to the ground floor.

'Off home?' he asked lazily as they walked towards the main door.

'Yes, if I can find a taxi.'

'A taxi? You mean ——'

'I don't have a car yet,' she finished for him, her tone rather lugubrious. 'And my hours don't lend themselves well to public transport. By hook or by crook I'll find something this weekend, because I'm spending a fortune in cab fares.'

'Your sister didn't leave you her car?'

'She had a little motorbike, which was fine for getting her back and forth between the house and the community health centre. But she sold it when ——' Hannah stopped abruptly.

'When they went to Queensland,' he finished for her.

'Yes.'

The subject had come up at last and Hannah wished fervently that she had seen it coming so she could have steered the conversation safely in the opposite direction. They were both silent, and when she saw a taxi pull up outside the front entrance to let off a passenger she broke into a run, hoping to hail it before someone else did, or before it left on another call.

'Hey! Stop!' Eden's voice came behind her.

'No, please, that taxi. . .'

'I know. Don't take it. For heaven's sake, I'll give you a lift. Melrose, isn't it? That's not far out of my way.'

She slowed and stopped. It was nice of him, but ——

The decision was made for her a second later when she saw a stout, elderly woman climbing into the waiting cab and realised from the droplets of water that misted the vehicle that it was raining. Windy, too. She heard the moaning sound of it through the automatic-opening doors in front of her. Two more people stood out in the front waiting for cabs, and the prospect of joining them didn't appeal.

'A lift would be nice,' she admitted. 'Thanks.'

'Wait here. No sense both of us getting wet.'

'I've just spent eight years in London, remember. I'm used to it.'

'But Londoners seem to have umbrellas that fold out of packets the size of a deck of cards. Either that, or they can grow new ones out of their sleeves at will. We Canberrans aren't in the habit of carrying such magic tricks around with us. Did you bring an umbrella today?'

'No, I——'

'Thought not. See you in a minute, then.'

He was gone before she could protest further and she was left to wonder about her mixed feelings as she stared out into the gathering darkness watching for his dark red car. On the one hand, she dreaded the possibility of Steve and Gina returning to their conversation. On the other. . . There was something very pleasant about the prospect of sitting in a cosy, purring car with him for ten minutes or so with a chance to talk on a more relaxed level. At work there was always so much medical business to discuss, and Eden Hartfield was thoroughly immersed in it. There must be another side to him, though. . .

'Damn it; I'm starting to like the man!' Hannah realised.

He pulled up seconds later and she climbed in, her dark halo of hair already silvered with rain.

'It's starting to come down quite heavily. You must be soaked,' she accused, then looked across at him and saw the dark patches on the shoulders of his shirt. He had removed his white coat as they crossed the foyer and now it was flung across the back seat.

'I'll put the heat on in a minute and we'll both get warm and dry,' he said.

'Mmm, yes,' she shivered suddenly, realising that she *was* cold. The neat black skirt she wore did not quite cover her knees as she sat, and she tried without complete success to pull it lower.

He switched on a fan as they curved down the hospital driveway, and warm air began to fill the vehicle. Hannah relaxed back into the cushioning cup of the bucket seat. . .and discovered that she was hungry.

'I missed lunch today,' Eden Hartfield confessed at almost the same moment.

'Not good,' Hannah scolded.

'And you? You managed a three-course sit-down meal in the staff dining-room?'

'Well, um — actually an apple and a couple of choc-olate biscuits,' she admitted.

'Thought so. You look as pale and hungry as I feel.'

'Oh, dear. . .'

'Sorry, that sounded rude. Pale skin suits you, with your dark hair and slate-coloured eyes.'

'Then I'll skimp on lunch more often. Anything for beauty!'

He laughed. 'Please don't! And to make sure that you're not going to try and skimp on dinner as well — yes, I saw that sheaf of medical journals you've loaded into your bag to read tonight — I'm going to take you home via a restaurant, where we can get some decent dinner.'

'Is that an announcement, or an invitation?'

'An invitation which I would urge you very strongly to accept. I can hear your stomach rumbling from here.'

'Oh, you can't!' For a momet she was horrified.

He laughed again. 'Perhaps it's mine, then. So take pity on me. I have no food in my fridge and I hate dining out alone.'

Should I protest any more? she wondered. But the words seemed to form themselves. 'In that case, I'd very much enjoy dinner.' And she found to her surprise that it was nothing more than the truth.

They dithered between pizza, Chinese and Thai, and finally chose the latter, although it meant a ten-minute drive in the opposite direction from Hannah's house. The restaurant was very quiet tonight, with only one other couple installed at a distant table, and the meal was more relaxing than Hannah would have believed possible ten days ago. She sensed that Eden wouldn't bring up the sensitive issue of Steve and Gina, and, when she tried to talk about work, he frowned that down as well.

'Thanks,' she told him. 'It's too easy to talk about it all the time, isn't it?'

So they talked about everything else under the sun instead. Their meal, Canberra's new and very magnificent parliament house, the holiday cottage that Eden had recently bought at a beach two and a half hours drive away on the coast. . .

'The beach!' Hannah sighed with sudden longing. 'It's years since I trod on good Australian beach sand.'

'You'll have to —' he began, then broke off, took a careful breath and finished ' — get down to the coast yourself this summer, then.'

'I'll certainly try to.'

'There are plenty of good places to stay these days,

in any category from three-star luxury to basic camping, all the way from Kiama to Tathra.'

It wasn't what he had started out to say, and they both knew it. She saw him put the half-full glass of wine he had been drinking further from his easy reach and was tempted to do the same with her own glass. It was a little frightening how well they were getting on together tonight — so well that he had almost issued a casual invitation to his new beach house, which she just might have accepted with equal thoughtlessness. How embarrassing that could have been in the cold light of day!

Looking up at him, she found that he was almost shovelling in the last piles of rice and fragrantly spiced chicken from his plate. No, not shovelling. There was nothing unattractive in the way he ate. . .unfortunately. Putting down his fork a few minutes later, he eyed her plate, which was not yet emptied, and said, 'Perhaps we should have opted for pizza, after all. I. . . I really didn't intend this to be a long meal. You had things to do this evening, and we both have surgery tomorrow.'

'It was the wine,' Hannah answered. 'Only a small glass each, but somehow that always slows a meal down.' She pushed her creamy beef curry around the plate a little more, ate a last mouthful and said, 'But I'm ready now, if you want to go.'

'Please. Finish your meal!'

'No, really. . .'

It was another fifteen minutes before they were back in his car, after a laughing dash through rain that was pouring down now, and she wondered if he was as sorry as she was that the evening was over. Those medical articles she had been planning to read held no appeal at all for some reason, and instead she had an absurd desire to go out dancing. An unlikely possibility in Canberra on a Tuesday night, and anyway, as he had pointed out earlier, they both had surgery tomorrow, beginning with a joint effort on Janice Peters' face and hand. . .

But the evening wasn't over after all. Eden had only just switched on his engine when the ultra-modern phone attached to the front dashboard began its electronic burr, and he picked it up with undisguised impatience. 'If I have to go back to the hospital. . .'

His manner changed as soon as he heard the voice on the other end of the line. His broad shoulders tensed and straightened, and fingers came off the steering-wheel to rake absently through the thick, dark weight of his hair. 'Yes, Sally, what is it?' And, after a pause to listen, 'Yes, of course, I'll come straight over.'

CHAPTER FOUR

EDEN turned to Hannah as soon as he had put down the phone, just seconds later. Knowing that she must have heard every word of his brief conversation, he didn't bother to explain.

'She didn't say what it was, but obviously it's important. She must have been trying me at home and at the hospital. Her place is just five minutes from here on the way to you. If I drop you home first, it'll take me an extra half-hour to get back to Sally's, but if we could call in on the way. . .'

'Of course, if it's urgent,' she assured him. 'Let's get going.'

They drove in silence, the mood between them completely altered now. Hannah couldn't help thinking of Gina and Steve living their carefree, determinedly futureless life together in sunny Queensland, while here on this cold, rainy Canberra night, Sally had to turn to her brother-in-law for help in an emergency.

Eden Hartfield's car splashed through streets that were flooding in parts now. He swore under his breath as they hissed through one long puddle that was deeper than it looked and dragged the car's wheels over to one side, threatening to skew the vehicle. Hannah held her breath as he straightened and controlled the steering-wheel. No real danger of an accident, but she saw that he was frowning heavily, and the frown did not go away as they drove.

As he had said, it only took five minutes to reach Sally's. 'Would you like me to wait in the car?' she offered as he pulled into a cracked cement driveway.

'Don't be ridiculous! It's unseasonably cold and the car will chill down in no time. I hope I won't be long, but I'm sure Sally will want to make you some tea.'

'I just thought ——' she began.

'I know what you thought. If you don't mind, I *won't* use your last name when I introduce you. Lombard isn't all that common, and I'm sure you don't want Sally making the connection between you and Gina any more than I do.'

'Yes, that's what I was wonder ——'

'Come on.' He cut across her words and Hannah followed him meekly up to the front door through the rain, both of them having to splash through muddy places where the lawn had died off and not been reseeded. Not a very tidy or well-kept garden, and that showed in a suburb where almost all the houses *were* well-kept in every way.

Sally had obviously been waiting. She opened the door before Eden had even poised his hand to knock, and barely seemed to noticed Hannah as she dragged her brother-in-law inside and pointed tearfully at the windows of the living-room.

'Look!'

At first Hannah couldn't see the problem. That rain certainly was teeming down in sheeets outside, making the glass look like a waterfall. Then she realised that the water was coming down the *inside* of the windows.

'I've used every towel in the house. The children should be in bed, but if I leave this for long it'll flood the whole carpet and ruin it. I can't afford to replace it. I can't afford to have the floorboards go mouldy or swell up. Steve didn't clean the gutters before he. . . left, and I've been feeling so ill with the baby, I haven't dared try to get up there. They're blocked by leaves and the water is backing up so far it's ——'

'I see the problem, Sally,' Eden soothed. 'There's a ladder, is there?'

'Yes, at the back of the garage. And here's a raincoat and a sou'wester.'

He put them on at once, then strode off to the end of the corridor where a door opened into the enclosed garage. 'Open the roll-a-door for me, would you?'

'I'll do it, Sally,' Hannah came in quickly, leaping ahead of the pregnant woman, whose abdomen was just beginning to swell with the coming child.

'Thanks,' Eden said. 'It'll be easier to bring the ladder round the outside.'

They went into the garage together and she un-fastened the big metal door and pushed it up. Eden was already behind her with the aluminium ladder, ready to duck out into the miserable night. Sally had disappeared back into the house and the sound of a child crying could be heard faintly above the drumming of rain on the garage roof. If anything, it was coming down even more heavily now.

'What can I do?' called Hannah as Eden shouldered the ladder and went out into the rain.

'Nothing,' he shouted back.

'But. . .a bucket? To collect up the leaves. I could empty it for you and——'

'I'm going to scoop the leaves out by hand and drop them on the ground. That's quickest, and I'll come back at the weekend to rake them all up once they're dry.'

'Right. . .' She trailed off, realising that he was right. All that mattered was getting those gutters to drain before the flooding inside got completely out of con-trol. She half closed the big garage door and went back along the corridor, to find Sally in tears now as well as the children.

'It's coming into the playroom now, and I haven't got a single towel left that's not soaked.'

'What about cloth nappies?' suggested Hannah. 'They're pretty absorbent.'

'Yes! I've got four dozen!' Sally turned on her heel, but Hannah stopped her.

'And if you have a washing machine I could spin-dry some of the sopping towels so that they can do a second shift.'

'Great! In here!' Sally pushed open the door of a laundry that was piled high with children's clothing, both clean and dirty, then left Hannah alone.

Hannah found two plastic buckets—useless for collecting water, as it was all running down the glass in a flat sheet, but perfect for filling with sopping towels.

For the next half hour she shuttled back and forth, spin-drying saturated towels, pressing them against the streaming windows again, and spin-drying the next lot. Soon, nappies from the playroom were soaked and had to go in the machine as well, then came the older boy Ben's announcement that his bed, lying beneath the window in his room, was wet as well.

'Tell poor Eden that he'll have to clean out the gutters on this side of the house as well,' Sally said, and then, surprisingly, she laughed. It did wonders for her tear-blotched face. 'Oh, this is so awful that it's funny, isn't it? That rain hasn't eased. Eden must be soaked. The boys are frazzled and now Ben can't even use his bed!' She blew her nose, then added, '*And* I don't know your name, you marvellous woman, to be helping like this.'

'I'm Hannah. Hannah L—*Hannah*,' she finished firmly. 'I—er—know Eden from the hospital.'

She was relieved to be able to escape outside to find him and tell him about the other blocked gutter.

'Go back; you're getting soaked already,' he shouted

at her when she found him and the ladder at the far
end of the house. She tried vainly to shelter beneath
the eaves.

'I just came to tell you that water's coming in on the
other side of the house as well,' she shouted back.

'Oh.' The news didn't seem to dampen his spirits —
an apt expression — although Hannah could see that he
was already utterly soaked. The sou'wester had blown
off — she found it, sodden and muddy, under some
leaves on the ground — so that his hair was plastered
down and streaming with water. The sleeves of the
raincoat were muddy, as were the blue shirt-cuffs
visible beneath. The lower half of his dark trousers was
so wet that the leg hems dragged down below his shoes.
But his voice was quite cheerful as he said, 'I'm almost
finished here. It's draining now. You should see the
flow tapering off inside very soon. Meanwhile, I'll take
the ladder straight round the back. Now go inside!'

She obeyed, and resumed her activity with the
towels. Sally was closeted in two-year-old Geoffrey's
bedroom, reading him a bedtime story and playing a
tinkling music-box as part of his night-time routine, but
four-year-old Ben followed Hannah back and forth in
a ghost-like way, 'helping', and wanting to know if he
would have to wear a raincoat to bed tonight.

Finally, at half-past ten, all was quiet and the flooding had stopped, although the rain still poured down
outside. Geoffrey was asleep in his own bed and Ben,
thinking this very exciting, had been settled on to a cot
mattress on the floor of his room, well away from the
damp walls and carpet beneath the window. His bed
had been stripped and the mattress was now drying in
the garage with the aid of an electric fan-heater
positioned a safe distance away.

Hannah loaded a last bucket of heavy, dripping
towels into the washing machine, switched it to the

spin-dry setting, then thankfully closed the door. Eden appeared at the door leading to the garage at that moment. He pulled off the muddy raincoat to reveal clothing that was almost as dirty and very messy.

Brushing dripping hair out of his eyes, he created a long muddy streak across the bridge of his nose as well. He had been working hard for well over an hour and his breathing came more heavily than usual, although you could never have said that he was panting. And somehow, with all this, there was something impossibly masculine, impossibly attractive about the state of dishevelment and mess.

'I can't come in like this,' he said. 'Look at me! Ask Sally if. . . Well, Steve must have left some clothes I can borrow.'

'Yes, I'll ask.'

'And borrow something of Sally's for yourself,' he added drily.

'What? Oh. . .' She looked down and realised for the first time how wet she was herself. All that loading and unloading of sopping towels. . .

The sleeves of her blouse stuck wetly to her arms and the fabric on the front of it was saturated too, making it look dark and much less opaque than she felt comfortable about. The way the red material clung to her breasts, revealing their symmetrical peaks in no uncertain terms, was horribly embarrassing.

'Yes, Sally must have something,' she gasped, and turned quickly on her heel.

Sally did—a mauve sweatshirt for Hannah and a grey tracksuit of Steve's for Eden. Feeling selfish, although selfishness was not her motivation, Hannah peeled off her own wet blouse as well as the damp bra beneath, dried herself ineffectually with a tiny scrap of hand-towel, and put on the sweatshirt before taking Eden's clothing to him.

'Is there a towel?' he said.

'You've got to be joking!'

'Of course. Silly question!' He turned and found a pile of clean rags on a workbench in the garage behind him and wiped the worst of the mud from face and arms, then began to unbutton his sodden shirt.

'I'll see if Sally needs any help,' Hannah said quickly, retreating from the corridor in some distress once again. The glimpse she had had of well-sculpted chest muscles covered in a pattern of dark hair had been rather disturbing.

'No, I'm fine,' said the other woman a minute later. Hannah had found her in the kitchen putting milk on the stove to heat for hot chocolate.

'Sit down!' Hannah scolded. 'You look exhausted!'

'Thanks. . .'

Eden appeared just as the milk was beginning to foam, and Hannah decanted it expertly into mugs containing chocolate powder. The three of them sat at the kitchen table, enjoying the blessed peace, warmth and dryness at last.

Eden's hair was still wet but it had lost that flat, streaming look and was beginning to spring up into soft waves again. He had missed a streak of mud on his neck, and Hannah felt an absurd, itching desire to wipe it off. The tracksuit was loose on his shoulders and short in the legs, but it suited him all the same.

Sally, meanwhile, took sips of the chocolate with a desperate pleasure that told Hannah this was the first moment she had had to herself all day. Perhaps Eden had noticed this, too. He said, after a silence, 'I don't think it'll look too bad tomorrow. No permanent damage. But you may want to get those gutters checked. Even when blocked they shouldn't drain back into the roof like that.'

'There's no point in getting it checked, Eden, since,

if there *is* a problem, I can't afford to have it fixed,'
Sally answered, her voice and face suddenly tight.

'But Steve would manage to ——'

'You know that Steve has never managed money
well, even at the best of times, and this *isn't* the best of
times. I found a credit card bill today from three
months ago. It had got stuck behind the desk somehow
and never been opened, let alone paid. I didn't even
remember we *had* a card from this company, although
it's in both our names. For household things we've
always used the credit cards that came through our
bank. So now, of course, interest on the bill has been
mounting up. . .and look at these charges!'

She took the bill from a sheaf of papers in a rack on
the table and thrust it across to Eden, who laid it flat
on the table to study it. Sally pointed out different
items, finding each one easily, although the bill was
upside down from her perspective. She looked as if she
had been memorising the thing all afternoon.

'Charges to all those take-away food places. Chinese
and pizza. Yet it's months since the boys and I had a
take-away meal. Quite a big amount billed by a jewellery store. Jewellery! And this. A compact-disc player.
Can you see a compact-disc player in this house?'

Of course Eden couldn't, but if he went round to the
house where Hannah was living, he would see a very
nice one, set in a special stereo cabinet in the living-
room. She was deeply uncomfortable about witnessing
Sally's distress and anger, and felt very guilty about
how much she had been enjoying the music of the
compact-discs, although she hadn't known until now
that the player had been bought with Steve's money.

'That woman!' Sally spat out bitterly. Hannah
remembered that Gina had used the same phrase about
Sally. 'Does she actually care about Steve at all, or is
she just using him because he's buying her expensive

presents? Presents that he, *and* I, and the *children*,
cannot afford! When we took out that big mortgage so
we could afford this nice house, I told him I thought
we were stretching ourselves too thin, but at least then
I thought I'd be there to help him budget properly.
The driveway needs fixing, and now the roof. You
know he's always been extravagant. . .'

Eden could only listen and soothe, and Hannah
could only drink her hot chocolate and try to be as
unobtrusive as possible. The other woman obviously
needed to get it all off her chest. She was pretty,
Hannah realised now, although stress showed in her
face. Petite and fine-featured, golden-blonde hair,
green eyes.

She reminds me of someone, Hannah thought. And
then it came to her in a flash who that person was. . .

'Your evening was ruined,' Eden apologised to
Hannah in his car twenty minutes later when they had
been able to leave Sally—calmer now—alone.

'Oh, for heaven's sake!' she told him impatiently.
'That's not important.'

They drove in silence for a while, then he said out of
the blue, 'Does Gina look like you?'

'No,' said Hannah lightly. 'Not a bit. Actually, she
looks very much like Sally. Perhaps that's what he sees
in her.'

He didn't answer, but she could see he was angry.
Let him stew in it! was her first thought, but it was
accompanied by a strange sadness and disappointment.
The issue of Steve and Gina threatened to spoil the
memory of their dinner together now and, yes, the
memory of that almost laughable drama over the
flooded house as well.

'And do you still feel that Gina is blameless in all
this?' he asked at last through a strained throat.

'No, I don't!' Hannah answered him. 'But is anyone

blameless? Even Sally. Perhaps she hounded Steve about every tiny bill. Even you. Gina certainly seemed to feel that your success as a doctor has been partially responsible for Steve's mediocrity.'

'Oh, I'm fully aware of that theory. But it's a little off the point, isn't it? Sally doesn't have any family here. They're all in New Zealand——'

'And Gina's family is in Perth. Except for me.'

'What's that got to do with it?'

'Several years ago in London,' Hannah began reluctantly, 'I had an affair with a married man.'

'Yes, you more or less admitted it when——'

'*Admitted* it?'

'All right. *Told* me about it.'

'When I first got involved, I had no idea that the thing could possibly be so drawn-out, so painful and so—for me—pointless. And there was no one to warn me. No one to turn to. Like Gina, everything I learned about myself and about relationships I had to learn alone. At the beginning, for me, it seemed easy. From the beginning, *before* the beginning, he. . .Patrick. . .' She said his name carefully and deliberately.

'Patrick,' Eden echoed in an odd tone.

'. . .had done as much as he could to convince me that his marriage was essentially over and I believed him. Why shouldn't I? Marriages do end. Divorce happens all the time. And I was naïve. Where a cynic, or a realist, would have seen cold-blooded procrastination, I saw honour; he was waiting until the moment when it would hurt his children least. Where a realist would have seen lies and lame excuses, I saw painful moral dilemmas and a man struggling to answer to too many demands. It took me almost four years to wake up to the truth, and in all that time I think my only sins were naïveté and blindness. And I think Gina is the same. The only difference is that Steve has actually left his wife. As I said, marriages do end. If it hadn't been Gina, wouldn't it have been someone else?'

'Possibly. Probably.' There was a pause, then he said, 'So what finally ended it?'

Thinking about Steve and Gina, Hannah didn't understand at first. 'Oh, you mean in my case?' she asked after several seconds. 'No one thing, really. It was an accumulation of a hundred little things.'

'Little straws. But which one finally broke the camel's back?'

'Oh. . .' She remembered suddenly. 'I found some concert ticket stubs in his coat pocket. A concert I'd been dying to see, and he had promised he would take me. But he had taken his wife and he obviously hadn't remembered which woman he had made the promise to. And I realised that if he couldn't even keep the two of us straight in his mind. . .'

'So that's your story. . .'

'Yes. I'm not proud of it. In fact, why the heck I told you. . . Because of Steve and Gina, I suppose. To convince you that there can be another side to it. Because we're both so mixed up in their mess. . .'

'No, not because of Steve and Gina,' he told her softly, and only then did she notice that they had pulled up in front of her house and he had switched off the engine. 'Because of this. . .'

He leaned across and pulled her into his arms and his kiss took her so much by surprise that at first she didn't even know whether she wanted to respond. Her body soon told her the answer. Somehow she had sighed against him, the soft, clean cotton of Sally's sweatshirt loose and warm against her bare skin beneath.

There was something very sensual about the casual fabric. As her mouth met his, she crumpled the grey cotton-knit that he wore in her hands, then slid them lower and found his skin, bared where the sweatshirt had ridden up a little around his firm waist. He smelt a little of eucalyptus leaves and mud, but tasted more strongly of chocolate. Was it this odd combination that was so delicious?

Somehow, her lips wanted to explore the question very thoroughly, and his own mouth seemed very willing to comply. His fingers traced the line of her jaw, then fell to her throat, then rose again to tangle lightly in her full halo of dark hair. Her hands, meanwhile, had not been able to stop their exploration of his back. Under the loose sweatshirt she found a dried streak of mud. Goodness knew how it had got there, but it felt gritty so she rubbed it away with the ball of her thumb.

Then she realised how deeply her hands were buried inside his clothing and started to pull them free but he groaned, 'Don't stop!' and she relaxed against him once more, massaging the taut, hot muscles of his back.

Sally's sweatshirt was too loose. Its waistband offered no protection at all. His hands had slipped beneath it now and he seemed to gasp at the softness of the skin at her waist. Then he moved higher to the heaviness of her breasts. At first, he merely nudged them from below with gentle, almost tentative fingertips, making Hannah incredibly aware of their weight and tingling fullness, then suddenly he cupped them completely, tracing with his fingers the deep cleft between and the hard nubs at their peaks.

She shuddered and arched away from him, lost in the magic of his touch. After all that work with the leaves tonight, his hands had a faint roughness now, but it was delicious.

'Hannah. . .' His voice was hoarse with the same desire that was pounding and tingling all through her, and, if this had been a bedroom instead of a rapidly cooling car on a cold wet night, they might both have had difficulty in calling a halt to what had flowered so suddenly between them.

So suddenly? No, Hannah realised as she pulled her fingers reluctantly away from his skin and brought them out into the naked air again. Not so suddenly, perhaps. Looking back, she could see the tell-tale signs now. Their awareness of each other this afternoon, standing side by side at the sink on the seventh floor. The warmth and animation of their dinnertime conversation. The way she had been so disturbed by the classic maleness of him as he stood in the garage doorway at Sally's, soaked from head to toe, breathless and streaked with mud.

'I'd better go in,' she said, breathless herself now. A part of her hoped that he would argue, pull her back into his arms again, resume that magical exploration of her breasts and her mouth, but he didn't.

'Yes.' It was a growl and it caught harshly in his throat, as if the words didn't want to come out at all. 'You'd better. It's late and we both have surgery on Janice Peters, first up.'

'See you at rounds before that.'

'I'll wait until you're safely into the house.'

'Thanks.'

'Thank *you*. For your help at Sally's. And your tact. And just *you*.'

He touched her cheek with the tips of his fingers in a last caress and Hannah fumbled for the door, panicked suddenly about how far this had gone in just one evening.

'See you tomorrow,' she stammered again unnecessarily, and fled up the path to the front steps. Behind her, as she unlocked the door and turned on the hall light, she heard his engine start, grow louder, then fade as he moved off down the street.

*   *   *

'That's about it. Thank you, everyone,' Hannah said, stepping back out of the bright pool of light that glared over the operating table.

She looked at Eden Hartfield and saw that he was finished already, as his procedure on Janice Peters's right hand had been simpler this morning than her own work on the woman's face. Often with such a procedure he would already be gone, leaving the final touches to a junior surgeon — someone in the final years of a surgical residency — but today one of the medical students had detained him with a question and he was answering it with a clarity and detail that had everyone at his side of the table listening intently.

Hannah, absorbed in the delicacy of her own procedure, hadn't heard a word of what he was saying until now. Actually, she had been far *too* absorbed in her work this morning, if such a thing could be said of a doctor in the middle of surgery. She saw Alison Steadwood give her a slightly reproachful, disappointed glance and remembered that the younger woman had been expecting a chance to practise her own skills this morning. Too late now.

'I'm sorry, Alison,' she said humbly. 'I. . .' What to say? Make up some story about an unexpected complexity in the operation which had needed her own more experienced hands? Blatantly untrue, though. The procedure had gone very smoothly and Janice Peters ought to be pleased with the results. That left only the truth — or a version of it. 'I got carried away and forgot about you.'

'That's all right,' mumbled Alison.

What else could she say? Nothing to Hannah, anyway. Probably the story would go round, though, that Hannah Lombard wasn't very generous with her juniors in surgery. Did all the interesting bits herself. Didn't give anyone a chance to learn.

Ironic, really, as Hannah was usually very generous in this way and prided herself on being so. The trouble was, she had been so determined to focus fully this morning, so conscious of the danger of being the least bit aware of Eden Hartfield working so closely beside her. She had gone overboard in the other direction, blocking out everything but the patient and the procedure too thoroughly.

Hannah sighed through her mask as she left the operating theatre, then pulled it off, and her cap, and fumbled at the ties of her green gown. A successful specialist had to develop that sort of mental control. She hadn't realised before that you could get too good at it!

Beside her, Eden was removing his own theatre clothing. As soon as the place was ready again, he would be returning for another operation, while Hannah would move down the corridor to Theatre Four to do a septoplasty. She would have a longer wait, probably, as Theatre Four was still in the hands of Canberra's top orthopaedic specialist and might remain so for another hour. . .

No, evidently not. The head theatre sister came up to her at that moment. 'Are you almost ready to go again?'

'I can be.'

'There was a Caesar scheduled now for Theatre One, but the woman delivered naturally last night so we're free and ready in there.'

'Equipment, too? I don't need a vacuum extractor, but I *do* need —— '

'We can get set up very quickly if you give the go ahead. You'll be out of here nice and early.'

'Yes, do go ahead, then.' The prospect of finishing surgery in time for a decent lunch was suddenly very appealing.

'Went well this morning, didn't it?' Eden said to her as they waited.

'Yes.'

'We just have to hope that her expectations aren't too high.'

'She'll definitely hate how it looks at first, but once the swelling goes down. . .'

They had said all this to each other before, but it was a safe subject, and successfully papered over their mutual awareness of what had happened last night.

I'm not ready for this, Hannah realised as she made her way along to Theatre One several minutes later. But it's happening. Or is it? Perhaps it was just a kiss, and it won't happen again.

Somehow, that seemed a much more painful possibility. . .

'Can I talk to you for a minute?' It was Eden, late that afternoon.

He had caught her in the kitchenette of the burns unit with coffee in her hand and a big wad of Danish pastry in her mouth. Someone had brought in a bag of them for the unit staff, and somehow the fact that Hannah had managed a more than decent lunch today didn't stop her from wanting to devour the largest and stickiest one. A heavy day of rounds, surgery and clinic hours always made her hungry. She swallowed quickly, almost choking on it, and said, 'Of course. Talk away. Not Sean, is it?'

'No, he's doing well and his flow sheets show as good a urine output as I was expecting. There's a lot of fluid draining from the wounds, though, so we're still keeping the IV input at a high rate. But no, it's not Sean.'

'Then. . .?'

'I spoke to Sally on the phone about half an hour

ago. She said that a nice cheque arrived by post from Steve today. So. . .thanks.'

'For what?'

'For taking on Gina's house to save them the double rent. That must be where the extra money has come from. I know you didn't want to do it. Sally would appreciate it, too, if I could tell her.'

'You're very fond of Sally, aren't you?' she said impulsively, then wished she hadn't.

He was looking at her quizzically. 'Is that a request for further information?'

'No, I ——'

'I'm happy to tell you, Hannah.' He made coffee for himself and chose a pastry from the white paper bag as he spoke. 'I first met Sally twelve years ago when she was training as an occupational therapist. We went out together twice. Then she met Steve. I was in my internship year, while he was coasting along as a third-year medical student.'

'Coasting? In medicine?'

'He's brighter than I am,' was Eden's comfortable assessment. 'He did as much as he needed to to get through, but no more. I was far too serious then for Sally. For any woman, probably. And seeing their relationship grow more intense made me realise that I couldn't afford that sort of involvement if I wanted to have a real career in medicine. Seeing them together. . . Well, I didn't mind about Sally. As I said, we'd only gone out twice, very casually. I liked her as a friend. But I *did* mind about what their relationship did to Steve's studies, and what his studies did to their relationship. There was a time when he talked about specialising, and he could have been brilliant in a field like orthopaedics, but then they decided to take off with back-packs and see the world for three years as soon as he'd finished his internship. He was just finding his feet again in his first year of residency when Ben came along, then that heavy mortgage when interest rates were high, then Geoffrey. Steve's wrong to blame my attitude for his mediocre success as a doctor. . .'

'But don't we often resent people who learn a lesson from *our* mistakes?' Hannah asked gently.

'You mean. . .?'

'Through his life, you saw the importance of not tangling yourself too much with other priorities when your career goals were so important. You avoided the traps that he now thinks he fell into.'

'That's a perceptive analysis, Dr Lombard.'

She laughed. 'An impertinent one, too. After all, I don't know you or Steve very well.'

'Don't you?' His blue eyes searched her grey ones. 'I'm starting to think that you know me better than I want you to!'

But he didn't mean this last thing. Everything in his tone told her that he *did* want her to know him at least a little better, and she wasn't surprised when he added in a low voice, 'Could we go out at the weekend? Saturday?'

'Saturday is entirely consecrated to the purchase of a new car, remember? But——'

'Sunday. . .'

'. . .would be lovely.'

'We'll take a picnic, then, go to Tidbinbilla Nature Reserve and re-acquaint you with the local fauna.'

'Oh, yes! And a hike, too, please. I've missed the smell of the Australian bush so much these past eight years.'

'Good! We can settle the details later in the week.'

Sister Evans came up at that moment with a question, and Eden moved casually away, taking a long pull on his coffee. Hiding her face behind the diminishing apricot pastry, Hannah watched him go, her heart

thumping with a disturbing rhythm. She really hadn't
expected this. Hadn't expected that either of them
would be able to get over their bad start together, or
over the barrier that Gina and Steve still provided.
Hadn't expected that Eden Hartfield would *want* to get
over it.

And to think that she would be looking forward to
Sunday so much. . .! It was a little frightening. . .and
very nice.

CHAPTER FIVE

THE car was pale silver-grey and had had one previous owner — not the salesman's favourite 'little old lady who only drove it to church on Sundays,' but none the less someone who seemed to have looked after the thing well, and had only put fifteen thousand kilometres on the clock. It was modest in size, a 1992 model, and had a manual transmission.

After looking at over twenty cars and test-driving nine of them, Hannah had written out her cheque for this one, signed the papers under the watchful eye of the salesman at the large and reputable dealership, and was now prepared to love this vehicle to death. She certainly didn't ever want to go through the angst of buying a car again, so this one had better repay her investment, love her in return, and never, *ever* break down!

She turned into the driveway, slid beneath the carport roof, switched off the engine and pulled on the handbrake, said, 'There you are, Tinkerbell!' in a satisfied tone, and realised with horror that she had just endowed the snappy little machine with a very silly name that would probably stick to it for the rest of its days.

'Tink,' she mused aloud as she picked up keys and bag and swivelled neatly out of the front seat. 'That's better. . . Tink.'

She said it again as she reached across to the passenger seat for her white coat. Going straight after Saturday morning rounds to the group of dealers all located along one main road a mile or two from the hospital had been deliberate. She knew that male car salesmen had a less-than-impressive reputation when it came to dealing with female customers. By stressing her status as a doctor, she had hoped to avoid the, 'Here's a nice one in pink, and the upholstery matches your eyes,' approach, and, with all but one of the salesmen, it had worked. Needless to say, she hadn't bought Tink from him!

Snapping smartly up the front steps on modest heels, she turned to survey the car one last time, feeling very satisfied. . .and very weary. A cup of tea. . .or perhaps something stronger. It was after five o'clock, and she had been out all day. Key in the lock, coat hung on a hanger in the hall cupboard. . .and she suddenly froze, her spine tingling, knowing she was not alone in the house.

'Gina!' Her heart, which seemed to have stopped beating for a moment, started again and she sagged against the cupboard door. 'For a moment, I thought——'

'You're home at last!' The young nurse smiled, yawned, then burst into tears.

Hannah dropped her handbag on the floor and cradled the reddening face against her shoulders. 'Does this mean it's over?' she whispered, and even as she asked the question she knew that she hoped it was. Disloyal? Realistic? Callous? Or kinder in the long run? She didn't know.

'No,' Gina was sobbing. 'At least. . . I don't know. . . I don't want it to be over. Just a few weeks ago—*two* weeks ago, when you came up, everything was so wonderful, and now. . . I just got on the bus yesterday to come down. I had to see you and talk. It was an impulse. I left a note for Steve. I'm so tired. That overnight bus trip is awful. I tried to sleep this afternoon, but I kept hearing cars in the street and hoping they were you.'

'Come and sit down in the kitchen,' Hannah soothed. 'I'll make you a cup of tea, and then something yummy to eat. How about that tuna casserole with cheese and egg and mushrooms and celery that Alice makes. You've always loved that.'

'I'm not hungry. . .'

Gina waved the suggestion away, but Hannah made the casserole anyway and the younger woman didn't even notice her sister's labours as she sat at the kitchen table drinking two cups of tea then a glass of wine and talking about Steve.

It was eleven when they went to bed after an evening of television, and, as Hannah had suspected, the casserole had disappeared quite rapidly. 'Thanks, Hannah, for all your advice and support,' Gina had said in the end. 'I'll go back tomorrow night, I think. It'll be another gruelling trip, but I don't want Steve to worry. You're right. We *can* make a go of it. We can get past a divorce, and all that awful stuff, if we really love each other. This thing is too important to let go of. You're so right.'

Was that what I said? Hannah wondered a little helplessly as she climbed into bed. Surely it wasn't!

Actually, she hadn't said much at all. Gina had done most of the talking, and had convinced *herself* in the end that going back, trying harder and being more patient was the right thing. Hannah's gentle, tentative input had all been in the other direction, and she knew that her tactful suggestions — too tactful, perhaps, since Gina didn't even seem to have heard them! — had all been made with the image of Sally and that flooded carpet in the back of her mind. Sally, the carpet, the children. . .and Eden struggling with the blocked guttering.

Eden! He was picking her up at ten tomorrow morning, and she had suggested that he come in for some brunch before they left. 'It'll be all right,' she insisted to herself half-heartedly as she rolled over. Suddenly the bed didn't seem as comfortable as it had been when she climbed into it so gratefully a few minutes before, and her sleepiness had vanished.

'It'll be *all right*. Gina may still be asleep. . . No, she'd hear conversation and come out to see who it was. I can't just pretend she's not here. Can I phone him in the morning and cancel brunch, say I'll be waiting for him at the kerb?'

An imperfect solution, but it would have to do, and at least the decision relaxed her into sleep. The only problem was that at nine the next morning when she picked up the telephone, he wasn't answering.

He's out shopping for picnic things. He's probably coming straight on here, she realised. And I planned on fresh croissants from that bakery in Tuggeranong. There's nothing else in the house. I used the last three eggs last night in the casserole and I *can't* give the man cold bran cereal for a special Sunday brunch! I'll have to go out, too, and hope that I can keep him and Gina on friendly terms. . .

It took longer than she had planned, even after she had enjoyed the shortest shower on record and practically dived into her clothes. The French bakery was crowded and she had to drive more slowly and carefully than usual as the new car had still not revealed all its secrets — one of which was the fact that the digital clock on the dash was eleven minutes slow. It was ten past ten, not one minute *to* ten, when she screeched to a halt in the driveway, and Eden's dark red car already stood in the street.

Ten minutes late. Not very long, really, but plenty long enough, it seemed. She could hear the raised voices even before she had opened the front door, and when she did open it and entered the front hall, every angry word from both of them was clear.

'Just what business is it of yours, anyway?' Gina was shouting.

She was still in her nightie and Hannah's dressing-gown. His ring at the door had probably woken her. Her medium blonde hair was unbrushed and she looked astonishingly young and pretty in the dishevelled state.

'It's my business because I care about Sally ——'

'Yes, so I've heard! If you wait long enough perhaps she'll stop snivelling over Steve and fall into your arms instead. She'd leave us alone then, stop draining us of every penny Steve makes and everyone would be happy!'

'Gina!' Hannah's horrified exclamation was totally ignored.

Eden ignored Gina's outrageous suggestion as well. 'And I care about Steve, too, although both you and he seem to have trouble with that idea.'

'Hannah!' Gina suddenly rounded on her older sister. 'Get this man out of your house!'

'But ——'

'Don't worry, Hannah; I'm going.'

'No, Eden, please. I've just ——'

He didn't deign to reply, just swept her with a cold look, ignored Gina entirely and stalked out of the house. For a helpless second Hannah watched him go then she said threateningly to Gina, 'I'll find out later how this started. Meanwhile. . .' She thrust the paper bag of croissants into her sister's arms. 'Eat them! It doesn't look as if anyone else is going to want them.'

Then she hurried out of the front door — conveniently left gaping — and caught up to Eden in the street beside his car.

'You didn't tell me she was coming,' he said, with a mildness that didn't fool her for an instant. Anger still blazed in his eyes and made every muscle in his body rigid.

'I didn't know. She was here yesterday afternoon when I got home with my new car. She was upset, was talking as if the relationship might be over —'

'But you soon convinced her to try again.'

'No! The opposite! Or I tried, but —'

'Not what she says.'

'She hears what she wants to hear. Please, Eden.'

'No, Hannah. I'm going home. I think that's best in the circumstances. Let's face it, anything that might have been able to happen between us is doomed. The other night was. . .nice.' His pause left time for the startling memory of his kiss to flood her once again.

'Yes, it was,' she managed.

'But when I found Gina here this morning it made me realise that there are too many conflicting loyalties at stake.'

'What are you suggesting? That I should have thrown her out of the house?' Somehow anger was the easiest and most comfortable thing to feel this morning.

'Don't be ridiculous!'

'I see. You just wanted me to alienate her totally by telling her I'd met Sally, and how wonderful and put upon she is, and couldn't Gina just do everyone a teensy little favour and —'

'We can't talk about this rationally at all, can we?' he came in heavily.

'No, we can't.' Her own voice was tight with the realisation that he was right.

'I'd better go,' he said.

'Yes.'

'Your new car looks good.'

'Thanks.' She managed a smile, but couldn't manage

to wait until he had got into the car and started the engine.

As she turned away, she saw a picnic hamper on the back seat, piled with small parcels that she knew would contain cheeses and pâtés. A long, crusty loaf of bread stuck out of the top and plastic containers of gourmet salads could also be seen. There was even bubbly mineral water, a Thermos for tea, and a bottle of wine.

He had gone to a lot of trouble, and she wondered who would get to eat that picnic now. Sally and the boys, perhaps. Or the pretty red-headed dietician that worked on meal-plans for patients all over the hospital. Hannah had noticed just two days ago the way Linda Jorgansen smiled at Eden when she greeted him. A surprise invitation from Dr Hartfield would probably make her day. . .

Biting her lip, Hannah fled up the path and in the door to meet the onslaught of her younger sister's fury. 'You don't mean to tell me you're going out with that man?' Gina hissed at once.

'Not "going out". Just a picnic,' Hannah said dully.

'That's going out! My God, how *could* you?'

'Just explain to me why on earth it's any of your business at all!' Hannah burst out, goaded beyond endurance. 'You're happy with Steve. If I happen to like Eden Hartfield enough to go on a picnic with him, a simple *picnic*, Gina, why is that suddenly some test of sisterly loyalty which I have miserably failed?'

'Because he's on Sally's side, of course. Which means *you're* on Sally's side, or you will be, soon.'

'There aren't any "sides". Am I the only one who sees that? Or if there *are* sides, there are about fifteen of them. Warm up those croissants. I don't want any. I'm going to have a shower.' She simply couldn't be bothered thrashing the thing through any more. She had wanted to know how the argument between Gina and Eden had started, but that seemed irrelevant now.

'You just had a shower an hour ago,' Gina accused.

'I'm having another one. And I'll probably use all the hot water.'

Hannah did, but didn't feel much better when she came out. The day passed slowly, with both sisters tense and testy with one another. Gina phoned the bus company and made a booking for a late afternoon trip to Brisbane, via Sydney, which would arrive at lunch-time the following day. They each ate a croissant or two — Hannah, at least, without much enjoyment — and then it was time to drive to the bus depot, which they did in silence for most of the way.

'Nice car,' Gina said as they crossed over Lake Burley Griffin on Commonwealth Avenue Bridge. There were people out on the lake today, in paddle boats and small yachts, and Black Mountain was reflected choppily in the water. But neither woman had scenery uppermost in her mind.

The car journey was nearly over and Hannah knew that Gina's comment was intended as a conciliatory gesture. Tired of the strained atmosphere between them, she met Gina halfway and said, 'Yes, and I've called him Tinkerbell. What do you think?'

'Him? Cars are meant to be female, aren't they? Like ships. It's traditional.'

'So? I'm defying tradition. This car is male, with all the attributes.'

'And a horribly prissy name.'

'That just happened. Beyond my control. Between friends, it's "Tink", of course.'

'Of course. Now, tell me about these male attributes.'

'Strong, reliable, protective. . .'

'That sounds like a description of *you*, Hannah, not your car.'

'Oh, I —— '

'Look, I know you're angry with me for spoiling your day with Eden.' Gina leaned across and touched Hannah's shoulder briefly. 'But believe me, you'll be thankful later on when you get to know him better.'

'Will I?'

'Yes! He's married to his work, Steve says. He'll never get serious with any woman. You'd have been hurt if you'd fallen for him in earnest.'

'Would I?'

'Honestly! But I'm sure. . . There wasn't really any danger of it, was there, Hannah?'

'No, no danger.'

'It was just a picnic? Good!'

Gina was beaming as she waved from the window of the bus half an hour later. Hannah waved back and thought, 'She's maddening. . .and good at heart. . . and riding for a major fall with Steve. There's nothing I can do about it. . .or about Eden. And I'm *tired*!'

But there were times when a doctor was not allowed to be tired, and this afternoon turned out to be one of them. It was windy as Hannah headed back to her car, and the bag she carried casually by its shoulder strap bumped against her hip as she hurried across the car park. She felt the hard, unyielding corner of her electronic pager knocking against her through the soft leather of the bag, and when it suddenly began to sound, she at first wondered whether it was faulty somehow and had been bumped into action by the bag's swinging.

She looked at the device and saw the phone number that had appeared on the small read-out panel. South Canberra's Accident and Emergency department. Quickly she turned and went back to the tourist bureau building, where the bus depot was located and where she hoped she would find a public phone in working order.

In luck, she was soon connected to the hospital, and heard the news within ten minutes of the disaster. A light plane had crashed on take-off at Canberra Airport, and at least six casualties were on their way in, with possibly more to come.

'Several of them are burned,' she was told. 'The fuel tank exploded just after everyone had left the plane.'

'I'm on my way.'

As she drove, she indulged in a brief, selfish moment of irrational thankfulness: Gina wasn't flying today! Then her mind leaped ahead to what she would face over the next few hours. Serious burn injuries, complicated undoubtedly by other traumatic injuries as well. That would mean a delicate balancing act between conflicting treatments in the hands of different doctors who couldn't always agree on what was best. And they were such a new trauma centre!

Just two months ago — less! — such patients would have been flown immediately to Sydney. Now Canberra had the facilities. . .but did it have the experience?

The scene was chaotic when she hurried into the Accident and Emergency entrance of the hospital ten minutes later, still wearing the casual mushroom-grey trousers and black and grey pullover she had planned for the cancelled picnic. The first ambulance had arrived, and a second one, with sirens screaming, was already pulling into the bay. Teams of doctors and nurses hurried back and forth with trolleys, stretchers, monitors, equipment for intubation, IV stands. . . The list went on, and information was flung about as it came to hand.

'It was a ten-seater plane, plus two crew. . .'

'One known fatality. Still two people unaccounted for.'

'Three ambulant. Another one with major full-thickness burns.'

'Yes, Dr Hartfield is here. Dr Reith is on his way from Sydney by car, but he's not in range at the moment for his pager or his phone, so he doesn't know about the crash.'

'We're trying him every five minutes.'

'Dr James is on his way in. We have two with multiple fractures; one of them with burns, as well.'

'We need another respirator.'

'What's the story from the blood bank?'

Two operating theatres had already swung into action, one staffed by an orthopaedics team and the other by a combined team of surgeons who were repairing internal injuries and a major fracture on the same patient at the same time. Hannah was called immediately to assess the extent of the injuries in the four patients who were now known to be burned. Central line IVs had already been set up on all of them, catheters and endo-tracheal tubes were in place, and large inputs of fluids had been started.

'We need to operate straight away on this man, for a hip fracture,' an orthopaedic resident told her.

'You can't,' was her blunt reply.

'But —'

'Not for at least forty-eight hours, probably longer. Look at these burns! He's in major burn shock, and surgery like that now, before he's fully resuscitated, would kill him.'

'But —'

'I mean it. Splint it, immobilise it, whatever, but we *must* treat the burn shock and we *must* have access to the entire burn area so dressings can be changed.'

A more senior surgeon appeared as Hannah

scribbled further orders for fluid treatment, Swan-Ganz catheterisation and pain medication, and urgently directed a nurse to cut away the rest of the man's clothing as major swelling of the burn areas was already beginning.'

'What's the problem here?' the surgeon asked.

'She says we can't operate,' the resident explained bluntly.

'You can't,' Hannah said once again.

'For the hip fracture? No. But the man may have internal injuries that could prove fatal if — '

'It's your "could" against our "will", Harrison,' said a smooth voice behind Hannah's right shoulder. Eden Hartfield. 'Look at this patient! Full-thickness burns, reaching down to tendon and muscle here on the left arm.'

'OK, you win,' the other surgeon said. The resident, feeling his junior status, had wisely retired from the conflict. 'If he dies, he dies on your turf.'

'He's not going to die, Harrison,' Eden returned grimly. The two doctors glared at each other, then Peter Harrison moved away to answer a summons from down the corridor. 'We need to get this one up to the unit as soon as possible,' Eden said to Hannah now. 'Go with him, would you? Stay there and co-ordinate things in the unit. I'll stay down here. Find out how quickly we'd be able to get a third dialysis machine up there if we need it. Two of these patients are strong candidates for kidney shut-down, and Sean Carroll is using one of our machines already.'

'I'm looking at the amount of eschar on our man with the broken hip,' Hannah said. 'He'll need eschar-otomy, won't he, in several places, to release the swelling beneath the eschar tissue?'

'Almost certainly, yes, possibly fasciotomy as well.'

This second surgical technique involved cutting even

deeper through the burned tissue to release pressure
and constriction on healthy muscle beneath. Some of
this work would have to be done tonight under local
anaesthesia.

She wouldn't be going home, Hannah realised.

The Charles McGowan Burns Unit was buzzing and
expectant when Hannah arrived, accompanying the
first patient. Extra staff had been called in so that each
of the new admissions could receive one-to-one nursing
care in the first critical days of burn shock and resusci-
tation. The heavy demand for nurses had stretched the
hospital's resources to breaking point, however, and
Sister Evans reported at once, 'There simply *isn't*
another nurse available for the morning shift tomorrow
who has any experience in acute burn management.
Sandy O'Rourke is away until Tuesday. . .'

'Anyone with intensive care nursing experience,
then,' Hannah said. 'Or anyone at all. There are plenty
of us to issue instructions. We have four badly burned
patients and we're a new unit. We can't afford to lose
someone who would have lived if we'd had our systems
up and running for longer!'

They all felt this way, and, as the hours passed, a
scene that had seemed dramatically disorganised at first
became far less so. Bruce Reith arrived. A third dialysis
machine was located. Nurses worked constantly over
the application of silvadene-impregnated gauze, an
anti-microbial treatment that helped to slough off the
burnt skin and to protect the raw layers beneath from
infection.

Eden Hartfield came up from Accident and
Emergency with the last patient, saw her settled into a
bed, then drew Bruce and Hannah aside to explode at
them. 'The trauma team has been consistently under-
estimating fluid needs, as usual. They talk about the
strain on the heart, but we have drugs that can draw

fluid off the pericardium. What we *can't* afford are the effects of too much fluid loss. Is this an issue we're going to be able to fight out and win?'

'In my experience, no,' Bruce Reith answered. 'It's on-going, and perhaps it needs to be. Getting the balance right is critical, and each patient is different.'

'You're right, I guess,' Eden sighed. 'I gave the OK to discharge three more people downstairs who had minor burns as well as other minor injuries. We'll see them on an outpatient basis to change dressings and assess their progress. How are we holding up at this end?'

'Good,' said Bruce.

'A little short-staffed,' Hannah came in. 'How about sending Janice Peters to a general post-surgical ward? Her case is routine now, as long as no one does the wrong thing with her dressings, and we can be very specific in our instructions about all that.'

'Good idea,' Bruce agreed.

Eden came in, 'Yes. We never thought we'd have eight beds occupied this soon. I'd send another patient to a different ward, if we could, but I don't think there are any candidates for that. Certainly not Sean.'

The little boy had stabilised well over the past few days, and, although his condition was quite serious, there was no longer much fear of unexpected complications. Chris Gardener and Glenn Hayes, too, were well on the way to recovery, but they needed the specialised care and experience that the burns unit could provide.

Half an hour later, Janice Peters had been moved, to her own relief as well as everyone else's. 'There are two bad cases, aren't there?' she asked Hannah just before she was wheeled away.

'Yes, I'm afraid so.'

'I could tell from the way there are so many people

in and out of those rooms. I. . . I was finding it hard. I don't have much memory of the first few days after my accident, and I don't *want* any memory of it.'

'No, of course you don't,' Hannah answered, feeling a strong empathy with the woman at last. She might have an abrasive, unattractive personality, but she was as human and vulnerable as anyone else. Touching the rather bony shoulder as an orderly pushed the wheeled stretcher past, Hannah added, 'You might have some pleasant company down on women's post-op. I hear there's a television actress there this week, after an emergency appendectomy, but I don't know her name.'

'Really?' Janice's bandaged face brightened. 'I wonder who it could be.'

An hour later — perhaps longer; it was hard to keep track of time — Staff Nurse Gretchen Older told Hannah, 'John Ewbanks will be ready for Theatre in a few minutes. Dr Hartfield has already gone down, but we've ordered in some pizza if you're hungry and want to grab a bit before you go.'

'No, I'm not hungry, thanks,' Hannah said absently, already walking towards the door of the unit.

She knew she *should* be hungry. Tired, too. But all that had gone. There was simply no time for it now. Somehow it was already nearly eleven and their most seriously injured patient was ready for escharotomy.

John Ewbanks, Gretchen Older had said. He had been identified, then. Only now did Hannah catch up with the fact. One patient's name still wasn't known, as far as she knew, and that meant the relatives had not been told. They didn't yet know what they were in for. This night, for all its drama and activity, emergency surgery and tense exchanges between different teams of doctors, for all its exhaustion, confusion, pain and dedicated care, was only the beginning.

Tossing aside what must be her sixth gown, cap and

mask of the evening, Hannah left the unit, aware as
always of the difference in temperature in the foyer
outside. The coolness was refreshing. Some people
waited on the couches grouped near the lifts and a
couple of them looked up at her with haggard, expectant expressions which she forced herself to ignore. She
knew that Bruce Reith and Nancy Evans had been
talking to some family members and would be talking
to them again when there was more to say. Meanwhile,
she and Eden Hartfield had to think about surgery and
nothing else.

'How did the debriding go on John Ewbanks this
morning?' Eden asked Hannah eight days later.

It was a Monday, not a day that she had regularly
scheduled for surgery, but with the extra load, and with
the importance of removing that eschar tissue step-by-
step from their most seriously injured patient, she had
been working overtime in Theatres this week. So had
Eden. He looked tired and pale as he sat opposite her
in the waiting room that served both their offices, and
Hannah knew that she must look as bad. . .if not
worse. She knew that she was positively slumping in
this couch, and the thought of a steady stream of
patients all afternoon was a little daunting just now.

But at least she was able to say, 'It went well,' in
answer to his question.

'I did the second of Sean's grafts this morning,' he
said next, 'and that went well, too. We've been through
a pretty thorough trial of our acute burn management
techniques over the past two weeks, and I think Bruce
is pleased. I certainly am.'

'Did you see the paper this morning?'

'No, why?' he asked.

'That journalist has done a very nice follow-up story

to his first two articles, talking about the plane crash and the way South Canberra responded.'

'Got a copy?'

'No, someone showed it to me in Theatres after surgery. Sorry.'

'I get the paper delivered at home. I'll see it tonight.'

'If you can prop your eyelids open long enough to read it!'

He laughed, recognising that it might be a legitimate problem, then a knock sounded at the door, cutting across the moment.

'What's this?' Hannah stiffened. 'Not a patient half an hour early?'

'I hope not. I hope very much that it's pizza.'

'Pizza?'

'I've been living on the stuff this past week. My fridge is quite bare. . .except that every time I open it I realise it's not bare *enough*. Something in there smells awful and I don't dare investigate to see what it can be!'

He paid the delivery man for the pizza while Hannah choked back her laughter and tried to ignore the appetising smell that was already wafting to her nostrils. Why hadn't *she* thought of ordering take-away? She was starving, but the noise of the staff dining-room hadn't appealed. Coming here to seek peace and a chance to catch her breath ready for the afternoon, she had found Eden, and now guessed that his purpose was the same as her own.

She watched him absently as he put the cardboard box on the table then went in search of a plate from the small store of kitchen things that their receptionist, Annette Kenyon, kept in a cupboard below the sink. He saw the direction of her gaze, brought back a second plate and had served her a generous, steaming, cheesy slice before she fully realised what he was doing.

'No, please, Eden,' she protested feebly, but he only pushed the plate closer towards her, clucking his tongue.

'Do you really want Annette to have to revive you halfway through the afternoon with a big splash of cold water in your face?'

'No. . .'

'Then eat!'

They both did, in silence, and it was the closest they had come to any kind of intimacy since that scene beside his car eight days ago — a scene that could scarcely be called intimate at all.

Several times since that day, Hannah had caught herself thinking about the might-have-been of that cancelled picnic, but then — depending on the time of day — sleep had overtaken her, or the lift had arrived at the seventh floor, or a nurse had come to her bearing a seriously ill patient's flow sheets for the past few hours ready for her to study. Probably for the best. No reason to dwell on the whole thing. He hadn't referred to it, and she didn't intend to.

They had worked well together since the plane crash had erupted so dramatically into the hospital's life, and that would have to be satisfaction enough. It *was* satisfying, too, she found. Although much of their specialised training had been done on different continents — his here and in America, and hers in London — they seemed to have very similar ideas, and sometimes second-guessed each other with uncanny accuracy.

As she watched him take a second slice of pizza, Hannah remembered what Gina had said, and how she had said it. It had been an accusation, really: that he was so wedded to his work that no intimate relationship could ever be important.

Perhaps it's true, she mused. And perhaps it's true of me, too. My relationship with Patrick wasn't exactly

★★★★★★ PLAY ★★★★★★★
£600,000 LOTTO!

★★★★★★★★★★★★★★★★★★★

NO COST... NO OBLIGATION...

NO PURCHASE NECESSARY!

IT'S FUN

IT'S FREE

FREE BOOKS! CASH PRIZES!

OFFICIAL RULES
MILLION DOLLAR
SWEEPSTAKES (III)

NO PURCHASE NECESSARY TO ENTER

To enter, follow the directions published. Method of entry may vary. For eligibility, entries must be received no later than March 31, 1996. No liability is assumed for printing errors, lost, late or misdirected entries.

To determine winners, the sweepstakes numbers on submitted entries will be compared against a list of randomly, pre-selected prizewinning numbers. In the event all prizes are not claimed via the return of prizewinning numbers, random drawings will be held from among all other entries received to award unclaimed prizes.

Prizewinners will be determined no later than June 30, 1996. Selection of winning numbers and random drawings will be under the supervision of D. L. Blair, Inc., an independent judging organisation whose decisions are final. Limit: one prize to a family or organisation. No substitution will be made for any prize, except as offered. Taxes and duties on all prizes are the sole responsibility of winners. Winners will be notified by mail. Odds of winning are determined by the number of eligible entries distributed and received.

Sweepstakes open to residents of the U.S. (except Puerto Rico), Canada, Europe and Taiwan who are 18 years of age or older, except employees and immediate family members of Torstar Corp., D.L. Blair, Inc., their affiliates, subsidiaries, and all other agencies, entities, and persons connected with the use, marketing or conduct of this sweepstakes. All applicable laws and

regulations apply. Sweepstakes offer void wherever prohibited by law. Any litigation within the province of Quebec respecting the conduct and awarding of a prize in this sweepstakes must be submitted to the Regies des Loteries et Courses du Quebec. In order to win a prize, residents of Canada will be required to answer a time-limited arithmetical skill-testing question to be administered by mail.

Winners of major prizes (Grand through Fourth) will be obligated to sign and return an affidavit of Eligibility and Release of Liability within 30 days of notification. In the event of non-compliance within this time period or if a prize is returned as undeliverable, D.L. Blair, Inc. may at its sole discretion, award that prize to an alternate winner. By acceptance of their prize, winners consent to use of their names, photographs or other likeness for purposes of advertising, trade and promotion on behalf of Torstar Corp., its affiliates and subsidiaries, without further compensation unless prohibited by law. Torstar Corp. and D.L. Blair, Inc., their affiliates and subsidiaries not responsible for errors in printing of sweepstakes and prize winning numbers. In the event a duplication of a prize winning number occurs, a random drawing will be held from among all entries received with that prize winning number to award that prize.

This sweepstakes is presented by Torstar Corp., their subsidiaries, and affiliates in conjunction with book, merchandise and/or product offerings. •The number of prizes to be awarded and their value are as follows: Grand Prize - $1,000,000 (payable at $33,333,33 a year for 30 years): First Prize - $50,000; Second Prize - $10,000; Third Prize - $5,000; 3 Fourth Prizes - $1,000 each; 10 Fifth Prizes - $250 each; 1000 Sixth Prizes - $100 each. Values of all prizes are in U.S. currency. Prizes in each level will be presented in different creative executions, including various currencies, vehicles, merchandise and travel. Any presentation of a prize level in a currency other than U.S. currency represents an approximate equivalent to the U.S. currency prize for that level, at that time. Prize winners will have the opportunity of selecting a prize offered for that level; however, the actual non U.S. currency equivalent prize, if offered and selected, shall be awarded at the exchange rate existing at 3:00 P.M. New York time on March 31, 1996. A travel prize option, if offered and selected by the winner, must be completed within 12 months of selection and is subject to: travelling companion (s) completing and returning of a Release of Liability prior to travel; and hotel and flight accommodations availability. For current list of all prize options offered within prize levels, send a self-addressed, stamped envelope (WA residents need not affix postage) to MILLION DOLLAR SWEEPSTAKES (III) Prize Options, Mills & Boon Reader Service, PO Box 236, Croydon, Surrey, CR9 3RU.

For a list of prizewinners (available after July 31, 1996) send a separate, stamped, self-addressed envelope to: Million Dollar Sweepstakes (III) Winners, Mills & Boon Reader Service, PO Box 236, Croydon, Surrey, CR9 3RU.

•U.K. equivalent prize values at the time of printing. Grand Prize - £600,000; First Prize - £30,000; Second Prize - £6,000; Third Prize - £3,000; 3 Fourth Prizes - £600 each; 10 Fifth Prizes - £150 each; 1,000 Sixth Prizes - £60 each.

Mills & Boon invite you to play

£600,000 LOTTO!

LOTTO CARD No:

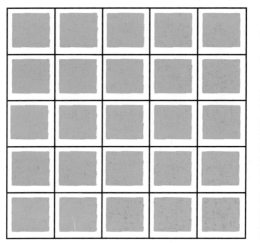

LOTTO SQUARES SCRATCH OFF

Instructions: Using a coin scratch away 4 or 5 silver squares in a straight line to see the maximum you could win in our Grand Prize Draw. 5 hearts revealed means this card is eligible for the £600,000 Grand Prize; 4 hearts revealed… the £30,000 First Prize; 3 hearts… £6,000; 2 hearts… £3,000; 1 heart… £600. VOID IF MORE THAN 5 SQUARES ARE SCRATCHED AWAY.

AND… YOU CAN CLAIM UP TO 4 FREE ROMANCES A CUDDLY TEDDY AND A MYSTERY GIFT ABSOLUTELY FREE.

To register your entry in the £600,000 Prize Draw and to claim your free books and gifts simply return this card. See the coupon overleaf for more details.

We are sure that once you have read your free books, you'll want more of the heartwarming Romances. So unless we hear otherwise, every month we will send you 6 of our very latest Romances for just £1.90 each. Postage and packing are free - we pay all the extras! Your satisfaction is guaranteed! You may cancel or suspend your subscription at any time, simply by contacting us. Any free books and gifts will remain yours to keep.

DON'T HESITATE REPLY TODAY!

FREE BOOKS CERTIFICATE

YES! Please send me the free books and gifts to which I am entitled and enter me in the £600,000 prize draw. Please also reserve a Reader Service subscription for me. If I decide to subscribe, I shall receive 6 brand new Mills & Boon Romances every month for just £1.90 each. If I decide not to subscribe I will contact you within 10 days of receiving my introductory parcel. The free books and gifts will remain mine to keep in any case. I understand that I am under no obligation whatsoever and that I may cancel at anytime simply by writing to you.

If you would like to enter the £600,000 prize draw but would prefer not to receive books please tick box. ☐

8A4R

Ms / Mrs / Miss / Mr _____

Address _____

_____

_____ Postcode _____

Signature _____

MILLS & BOON READER SERVICE
FREEPOST
P.O. BOX 236
CROYDON
SURREY
CR9 9EL

NO
STAMP
NEEDED

a success. As for Eden's and my attempt to. . . Inevitably, she remembered his kiss and her feeling of heady anticipation about the simple picnic and hike he had proposed. Well, that didn't get off the ground at all. I'm glad, too. This was very firm. Like this, we can be successful as colleagues with nothing getting in the way. With this attitude held deliberately in the forefront of her mind, she said lightly to him, 'Pass me that magazine, would you? I'll catch up on the latest Hollywood scandals for ten minutes, I think.'

'Good idea,' he answered solemnly, handing the glossy pages across. 'And a very important part of patient management. Distract someone with a provocative comment about what Elizabeth Taylor wore to the Oscars and you could probably amputate without anaesthesia and they'd never notice. Perhaps I should crib up on the subject, too. What *did* Elizabeth Taylor wear to the Oscars?'

He ducked and cowered back as she flourished the magazine at him in a threatening manner, and they both ended up laughing far more than the occasion warranted, intriguing a well-groomed Annette Kenyon who entered at that moment. It felt. . .nice.

But, if Hannah was looking for anything more than 'nice', she knew that, as far as Eden Hartfield was concerned, at least, she would have to look elsewhere.

CHAPTER SIX

'YOU haven't seen my lad since yesterday morning, have you, Dr Lombard?' Night Sister Sandy O'Rourke said to Hannah at half-past six on a Friday morning one long, busy and tiring month later.

The practical, very square-cut brunette often referred to her favourite patient of the moment as 'my lad' or 'my lass'. In this case it was John Ewbanks who had earned the endearment, and Sandy glanced in at him as she spoke. Following the look, Hannah could see that the thirty-five-year-old businessman was asleep, much of his skin still covered in dressings and his broken hip in a cast, but substantial parts of him now showing the red, meshed look of recent grafting.

'I think you'll see a big change in him,' Sister O'Rourke went on.

'You mean. . .?'

'The light's clicked back on.'

'It has? Terrific! That's a big milestone.'

'He's dying to talk. Will you be extubating him soon?'

'I was going to wait until after the next lot of grafts next week, but if he is fully alert now. . .'

'For the sake of his morale. . .'

'There's certainly a case for doing it today.'

'He scribbled down quite a bit yesterday, and tried to mouth things, but was obviously finding it very frustrating, according to Nancy Evans. His right hand is damaged, of course, and he could only work at it very slowly. Some of what he wrote was illegible.'

'Yes, that must be hard. We'll discuss it during rounds. I won't wake him now.'

She would have liked to. It was almost always a very clear and encouraging sign in a serious burn patient when he or she 'clicked back on', as Sandy O'Rourke had phrased it in her colourful yet down-to-earth way. Doctors still didn't fully understand why such patients so often spent the first days or weeks after their accidents in this state that was almost like coma.

Medically, it *wasn't* coma at all, yet relatives asked about it all the time, and it was easy to understand why. 'He's in a coma, isn't he?' Kerry Ewbanks had asked more than once as she looked at her badly injured husband, who was lying there so inert and unresponsive, with so little apparent awareness of where he was and what was happening.

There were moments of response and awareness during this time, particularly, of course, response to pain, in spite of the high doses of medication, but it usually wasn't until the last of the leathery eschar tissue had been removed that a patient emerged properly from this state.

'It's as if that dead skin is poisoning their system somehow, and when it's all off, they're not poisoned any more and they snap out of it,' nurses had said to Hannah in the past. It seemed as good an explanation as any.

The unit's other patients were all doing well, too. Chris Gardener and Glenn Hayes had been discharged, and Sean Carroll would be within the next few weeks, although all three would need to return at a later date for follow-up surgery. Hannah was enjoying the side of her work that did not involve burn patients, as well. Reconstructive surgery to the face and other areas of the body was always intensely satisfying. Repairing damage caused by accidents, correcting congenital malformations, removing scar tissue. . . Her patient load was beginning to build as she received referrals from other doctors in the area.

Janice Peters had now received what they hoped would be the last of the operations to her hands and face, and both Hannah and Eden were pleased with the results. So far, her personal life had not improved, though, and she sometimes talked unrealistically about flying to California for the sort of cosmetic surgery which she wrongly believed would give her a model's face.

She had come in for an office appointment last week, in fact, wanting a referral or at least a list of names. But Hannah had skilfully deflected these fantasies and had found out that Janice was pleased with the counsellor that Anne Gallagher had recommended, and whom she was now seeing weekly.

'Do keep seeing her,' Hannah had urged. 'And, if you have any problems or questions, please don't hesitate to come and see me again, too.'

And that was all she could do for her, she realised.

John Ewbanks was a different story. He had already shown a strong will to live, and now that he was suddenly so much more alert there was a strong case for removal of the tubing through which he had been fed for the past month. Hannah presented the idea to Eden before rounds began and he nodded thoughtfully.

'I agree that for his morale it would be good, and we can handle reinserting it for surgery, but what about the calorie intake?'

Most burn patients suffered from appetite loss, and at a time when their bodies needed a calorie input that was two or even three times higher than normal.

'We can supplement with TPN intravenously,' Hannah offered. The abbreviation, which both she and Eden were very familiar with, stood for 'total parenteral nutrition'. She went on, 'John is compliant and well-motivated. We'll be able to make him understand the importance of eating.'

'Linda Jorgansen can talk to him about it. She usually gets very good results,' Eden said thoughtfully.

Hannah couldn't help watching his face. She was sure by this time that the dietician was not simply impressed by Eden Hartfield as a doctor. . .but how did he feel about her? None of her business! Firmly, she pushed the subject from her mind.

'John's family support is good, isn't it?' Eden was saying, using the patient's first name easily and unconsciously. This was one ward where the custom of always addressing patients formally had broken down. The relationship between staff and patients was often so intense here, and lasted for so many months, that it seemed important, somehow, to break through the conventions.

'His family support is *very* good,' Hannah came in. 'Kerry is in virtually every day, sometimes twice, and if ever she can't make it she lets the nursing staff know and checks to see that someone else *is* coming. John's brother, or his cousin, who both live in Canberra. She gets the children to make tapes for him, with singing and stories about what they've been doing.'

John's children were only six and eight, and no children under the age of sixteen were permitted as visitors in the unit—a hard rule, but a necessary one for several reasons, including the danger of passing on infection.

'You've seen the drawings and collages on the walls,' Hannah went on. 'The children did those.'

'Would his wife bring in food for him?' Eden asked. 'A home-cooked meal, or his favourite take-away food might tempt him more than——'

'I'm *sure* she would. Three meals a day if we told her it was necessary.'

'Then let's do it.'

Alison Steadwood performed the simple extubation procedure an hour or two later when Eden had already gone down to Theatre for his regular Friday morning surgery and Hannah had crossed an open, grassed area to a different building where she held an outpatient's clinic on Friday mornings, doing follow-up work or minor treatments on a variety of patients.

It was usually an easy, pleasant morning, and today was no exception. Plenty of time to notice the November sunshine through the window and to wonder how Eden's grafting and debriding work was going with the other seriously burned plane crash victim, Joan Tate. Although less extensively burned than John Ewbanks, the older woman had not been in such good health to begin with, and her road to recovery had been very rocky, and still was. Heart, liver and kidney specialists had become involved in her treatment, as each of these organs had been stressed by burn shock, and each attempt at surgery had to be made with great caution, with the danger of complications a very real one.

But when Sister Evans phoned down from the burns unit just as Hannah's last patient had departed, slightly late, at the end of the morning, it was with news of John Ewbanks, not Joan Tate. 'I think you had better come up,' Nancy Evans said. 'He's very upset and he's asking for a mirror to see his face. He's pulled out his IV.'

'Deliberately?'

'No, an accident, but it came when he was thrashing around more than I've ever seen him do before.'

'He's started to realise just how badly he was burned,' Hannah said. 'And he's an intelligent man. He'll be thinking about all the consequences. . .'

'He'll have questions, too.'

'A thousand of them. I'll come straight up.'

Nancy Evans met Hannah at the door of the unit and spoke quietly to her as they crossed the floor together. 'He's much calmer now, and we got the drip back in. He apologised for making it come out. . .but he still wants a mirror.'

The injured man did not try to move when Hannah entered the small room that was still so crowded with monitors and other equipment. His bed was partly raised at the head so that he was in a semi-reclining position, and he could easily look her in the eye. He seemed to want to do this, and spoke at once, very forcefully, as if he wanted to signal that he wasn't going to be fobbed off with chat.

'You're going to tell me to be reasonable and sensible, aren't you?' The words were a little distorted, as his face had been partially burned, including the top of his head and much of his hair. It would be a long time before grafting and cosmetic surgery could restore his facial appearance, and before the scar tissue faded from mottled red to a paler colour that matched his skin tone. But he was alive and it was clear that he was glad of this.

'That depends,' Hannah answered him. 'Perhaps you're being reasonable and sensible already.'

'Nancy doesn't think so.'

'What do *you* think? What's on your mind?'

'I've been in a funny kind of state since the car accident. It's been days, now, that I've been here, hasn't it?'

'Weeks,' Hannah amended gently. 'And it was a plane, not a car.'

'A plane? That's right. I was flying up to Dubbo to look at a property. Somehow, I thought we never got to the airport, but —'

'Don't try to piece it together,' Hannah advised. 'It's

a kindness our bodies and minds do to us sometimes. They want us to forget.'

'Then I was pretty bad. . .'

'For a while.'

'I can remember wanting to help. People were telling me something was going to hurt, but I believed them when they said it would do me good, so I tried to keep still. I knew. . . I believed in all this,' he waved his hands at the monitors and tubing that still surrounded him.

'Yes, you've been very co-operative in all your treatment,' she told him.

'And when it *did* hurt, I'd ask for something for the pain, and someone would give it to me. Am I addicted now? Is that why I've been so unaware? Perhaps my dosage should be ——'

'You're still in pain. Don't try to be heroic. Pain is exhausting and trying to battle through it could slow your recovery.'

'Kerry comes to see me a lot, doesn't she?'

'Every day.'

'What does she think of it? I've hurt my face, haven't I? I want to see it, and the other parts of me. I can feel bandages everywhere and I want to know, I want to *see* which. . .bits. . . I have left. Listen, are you my only doctor?'

'No, but ——'

'Who's that man I see? Dark hair, blue eyes that make you think of the sea on a sunny day.'

'Eden Hartfield.' Not hard to recognise the description! 'Yes, he's a doctor, too. You've sustained some damage to the tendons and muscles in your hands. Later on he'll be working to restore those to normal function.'

'Can I talk to him?'

For a brief moment, Hannah was angry. She was

female, therefore she didn't count. Was that it? Then she realised that that was *not* it. John Ewbanks wanted to know about the physical side of his marriage, and his wholeness as a man, and Hannah sensed that this meant more to him than a simple reassurance that certain parts had escaped the searing heat of the exploding flames that day almost six weeks ago.

She could tell him breezily that physically there should be no problem, but then he'd just nod and say nothing more, be too shy, with a strange woman, to keep on probing, while underneath. . . He *did* need a man.

There was a male nurse on this shift. Short, solidly built Alan Hammett was nice, but a little brash and a little too fond of the kind of sexual innuendo that would *not* suit John's mood today. He needed Eden.

She said aloud, 'Of course you can talk to him, but possibly not straight away. He may still be in surgery.' She saw the disapppointment etched crudely on the injured features and added encouragingly, 'But your wife often comes at about this time.'

'Kerry? I don't want to see her.'

'But——'

'I *don't* want to see her, I tell you!' His voice was raw and grating and he moved violently in the bed, without stopping to think, then cried out in pain at the disturbance of one of his dressings and the still-weeping skin beneath. A monitor was tripped into action and gave off its electronic warning signal.

Sister Evans appeared in the doorway with eyebrows raised. Hannah shook her head, and went across herself to straighten out the kinked tube that had set off the signal, but John had already seen the senior nurse. 'I'm issuing some instructions,' he said harshly. 'Kerry Ewbanks is not to be admitted into this unit to see me until further notice. She has bad intentions towards me. And I need to see a lawyer. Kerry Jane Ewbanks of 18, Curtin Crescent, Playford is to be refused all access to bank accounts and credit cards in my name, and I will not be responsible for her debts.'

'All right, Mr Ewbanks,' Sister Evans said, wisely choosing to address him more formally on this occasion. 'We'll get someone to see to it all straight away.'

She exchanged a look with Hannah. Poor John! And poor Kerry. The man was not mad, as he might seem to an outsider. This phase was common enough in patients emerging from a burn-shock induced fugue state, and in patients emerging from many other kinds of unconsciousness too — full coma, stroke, aneurism. Characterised by a degree of delusion or paranoia, it could come on very suddenly, be disturbing to witness, and sometimes be difficult to navigate through tactfully, but it rarely lasted long. Within a day or two, or even less, he might forget that it had ever happened.

The doctor and nurse moved out of John's earshot, relieved that he had quietened now and had seemed to accept Nancy Evans's answer to his wild demands.

'Kerry might be waiting outside already,' the nurse said.

'I know. I'll go out and talk to her. This is stemming partly from his fears that she is going to reject him physically, or that he'll be physically inadequate. He wanted to talk to Dr Hartfield. I don't know if now is the right time, after all, but. . . Could you page him?'

'He should be on his way up,' Nancy said. 'Joan is back from Recovery, and he wanted to see her. He just phoned to say he had finished the two carpal tunnel releases he had scheduled.'

'If I don't meet up with him in the foyer——'

'I'll tell him, of course.'

Emerging into the seventh-floor foyer, Hannah

couldn't see Eden Hartfield, but she saw Kerry at once, and the neatly built brunette — about Hannah's own age — stood up at once, dropped her magazine and came forward.

'Hello, Dr Lombard! Are they ready for me in there?' She was as cheerful and eager as always, obviously very much in love with her husband, and it was hard for Hannah to break the news.

'I don't think it's a good idea for you to see him today, Kerry,' she said gently.

'Not see him? But —— ' Her face paled immediately and she clutched the air for support. Cursing herself, but not knowing how else she could have begun, Hannah took the woman's arm and steadied her.

'He's fine,' she said quickly. 'This is progress, but I have to warn you that it won't seem like it.'

'He was so alert yesterday evening.'

'He's still alert, but he's experiencing a very common and very *temporary* state of confusion.'

'Confusion? You mean amnesia?'

'No, not amnesia. Paranoia, I guess, is the best term. He's anxious about your response to him, now that he's aware enough to realise the extent of his injuries, and at the moment that anxiety is taking the form of hostility. He has given instructions that you are not to be admitted, and are not to have access to his finances.'

'Oh, oh, *no!*' She had begun to tremble.

'It's *temporary*, Kerry,' Hannah insisted. 'It's not real. But beneath it there *is* some genuine anxiety, as I said. In this state, it's best if we do keep you away, but when you see him again, which may be as soon as tonight, please try to reassure him — not with words, perhaps, but with your manner — that your feelings are still the same.'

'But what more can I do?' Suddenly the injured man's wife was sobbing and finding it almost impossible to speak. 'What more, Doctor? Of course my feelings are. . . I've been here. . . Hasn't he known me all this time? Does he think I haven't been coming?'

'No. . . I'm sorry. I've upset you.' Hannah cursed herself once again, and once again did not know what else she could have done. 'All I wanted to do was to urge you to express it more, to ——'

'I don't know. . .how. . . I can. . .' The sobs were shaking Kerry so much now that Hannah put out her arms and just held the woman without speaking for several minutes, feeling rather overwhelmed herself.

She had seemed to be handling it so well. They both had. Hannah thought. But now they've both gone to pieces and I wasn't prepared to be the one to catch them. It was too easy, Hannah knew, to let the nurses handle the most human, tender side of patient care, particularly in a period like now, since the plane crash, when their new unit was so suddenly operating at top speed, and its doctors were so involved in more technical decisions: how much to debride in one operation; what grade of meshing to use in a skin graft; how to improve kidney function. . .

I have to let this run its course, Hannah decided. I won't get lunch before office hours this afternoon, but too bad! This is far more important.

Soothing the woman, and walking with her back to the lifts, Hannah did not see Eden emerge, take in the scene, and move rapidly towards the burns unit door. It was fifteen minutes before Kerry Ewbanks was completely calm. Red-nosed and puffy-eyed, she gave Hannah a muffled thanks through the mask of a sodden handkerchief.

Hannah replied, 'Try again tonight. Ring the unit any time during the afternoon and Sister Evans or Sister Older will tell you how he's been.'

'Mm-hm,' Kerry nodded, calm now, but still snuffly.

Some other people were waiting in the grouped chairs: Sean's mother and aunt; Joan Tate's husband. They all knew each other by this time, of course, and could sometimes provide each other with support, a listening ear, or just someone to chat to, but now was clearly not the time, so everyone kept their distance as Hannah escorted Kerry towards the lifts.

'Sit down for a while in the cafeteria and have some tea,' the doctor advised. 'Don't try and drive until you're feeling a little better.'

'Thanks. You're right,' Kerry sniffed again.

As the lift doors closed on the other woman, Hannah thought, That's good advice for me, too, coffee or tea. She looked down at her wristwatch. Twenty minutes until office hours over in the other building. Back to the unit, in that case, she supposed. She might find a biscuit or two there.

But, standing at the sink starting to wash her hands, Hannah didn't look forward to a snatched cup of tea in a place where patients and their needs were bound to swamp her once again. Reaching aimlessly for a paper towel, she stood with it crumpled in her hands, thinking, I wonder why this has got me so drained. I've seen patients in delusion and their relatives in tears before this.

But not after so many weeks of extra work and stress, she realised. Flying from London, getting settled, the new job, Steve and Gina and Sally, the plane crash. . .and Eden Hartfield.

I can't do it, she thought. I can't go back in there now, among the pain and problems and monitors and demands and decisions, and calmly make a cup of tea. Not if I want it to do me any good! I'll go. . .anywhere! Outside. Fresh air.

'Who are you seeing?'

The door had opened and Eden had asked the

question before Hannah could even throw away the paper towel still crumpled in her hands, let alone pick up her white coat and leave.

'Oh. . .no one,' she stammered stupidly, aware that her voice trembled slightly. 'I was going to go in and grab some tea. Then. . . I changed my mind.' He had loomed beside her far too suddenly, and she was aware of him in a way she had not let herself be for over a month.

'Mrs Ewbanks has gone, then?'

'Yes. She was pretty upset.'

'I saw the two of you as I came through.'

'Did you talk to John?' She had to hear about it now, although she didn't want to.

'Yes. I reassured him about his physical abilities. I told him that emotionally he could take longer to feel like a normal male again, but that that *was* normal for someone who'd been through what he has been and will be going through. And. . .'

'And?' she prompted, again with effort.

'I showed him his face.'

'*What*?'

'He needed to see it. From the way he was talking, it seemed to me that he was actually imagining it was worse than it is. He's an intelligent man. He told me he'd seen pictures of burn victims before, and if he looked like that, then he wanted to know it. He *doesn't* look like the worst cases, which you know as well as I do. One side of his face was almost completely untouched. So Sister Evans brought a mirror and we showed him.'

'And?' she prompted once again.

'He took it well. Told me Kerry had always thought he had a handsome profile, and he was glad that it, at least, was still ninety per cent intact.'

'No mention of the delusions about Kerry?'

'Obliquely. Said he needed to apologise to you and Nancy, that he'd got angry and lost control a bit, and was looking forward to seeing Kerry tonight. Wanted to ring her to make sure she was all right because she hadn't come in. I didn't tell him she *had* been in and he'd refused to see her.'

'Mm-hm.'

'Are you all right, Hannah?'

'Fine. A bit tired, that's all.' Suddenly she was finding the cramped space beside the sink more than a little claustrophobic.

'The shoulder of your blouse is wet.'

'From Kerry's tears.' She managed a smile, noticing the damp patch herself for the first time.

'Here. . .' He reached for a paper towel and pressed it to the dark green cotton. 'It won't do much, I suppose, but. . .'

'Thanks. It's all right.' Gently but firmly she pushed him away and reached behind her for the white coat which she had hung temporarily over a peg.

His touch and concern had disturbed her at once and she wasn't going to give in to the feeling. . .except that holding herself stiffly like this only seemed to be making her feel more weak and shaky than she had been already.

Eden crumpled the towel and held it in his hands, watching her narrowly and seeming uncertain for a moment. Uncertainty. It wasn't an attitude she often saw in him. . .and it didn't last long. Suddenly the paper towel was tossed into a bin and warm arms had encircled her.

'Hannah, don't push me away,' he murmured, his voice caressing through the fall of her hair. 'You look as if you're at the end of your rope. Tell me about it, please!'

'It's nothing. It's stupid. I——' She couldn't go on, and she couldn't let him go, either.

It wasn't tears that threatened to overwhelm her but sheer weakness and she knew that if he didn't keep his strong arms about her like this she would have to reach for the sink for support and lean ignominiously over it. Eden's warm male strength was far nicer than the hard stainless steel of the sink's rim.

'Hey! It's all right. It's all right,' he crooned in her ear, his hands slowly and rhythmically chafing her back.

Burying her face in his neck, she could smell his woody aftershave and feel the soft prickles of shampoo-scented hair that ended there in short, loose waves. His hard thighs pressed against her own softer ones through the full fabric of her printed cotton skirt, shoring her up with their strength, and slowly she felt the power of her muscles returning.

When, after several minutes, his warm palm slid along her jaw to coax her face towards his kiss, she was not surprised. Her own body had begun to urge her into a more sensuous kind of touch. For what might have been many more minutes, her lips responded to the exploring and increasingly demanding pressure of his mouth. It was so unexpected, so delightful and rich and alive. His nose grazed hers as he tilted his head, and his fingers plaited tingling strings of awareness at her throat before sliding down across the fullness of her breasts towards her far slimmer waist.

And she knew it had to end. Not because she was due at their office five minutes' walk away, not even because at any moment someone might walk in here and spoil the intimacy of their kiss with a prying glance, but because with every second of his touch he was undoing all the work she had had to do over the past month and more—the careful way she had told herself that that first kiss had meant nothing, that it was all for the best, that he was wedded to his work and so was she.

It hadn't been too hard to tell herself all those things the first time, but she already knew that this time it *would* be hard. Since the plane crash and the picnic to Tidbinbilla that hadn't happened, they had had nearly six weeks of working intensively together, making decisions that had literally saved the lives of John Ewbanks and Joan Tate and made life worth living for many other people. Six weeks of seeing their new unit settle into an efficient and yet very human routine. Six weeks of sharing a snatched lunch, comparing notes at the end of an afternoon in clinic or the office, agreeing over surgical issues. Six weeks of *disagreeing*, sometimes, and thrashing that out with a mixture of humour and heated debate. Six weeks, too, of *not* talking about Gina or Steve or Sally unless they absolutely had to.

I was kidding myself, Hannah realised. I thought I'd nipped it all in the bud, but really everything was flowering away under the surface and now his kiss is ten times more powerful than it was that first time.

At last she managed to drag her mouth away, although his lips followed her movement hungrily and a groan broke from them when finally she was free, pressed back against the hard rim of the sink, staring down and breathing deeply. She wanted to say something that would put a safe lid on this, would keep it from happening again, but words would not come.

'I'll be late,' was all she could finally manage.

'I have a meeting,' he growled in reply. 'I was late fifteen minutes ago.'

She took her coat and draped it over her arm then left just ahead of him, very thankful for the cooler air of the foyer. His meeting, hopefully, was in one of the conference rooms on the tenth floor and they wouldn't have to share the lift. Reaching the controls, she pressed a 'down' button, then felt his sleeve brush hers as his hand came past to seek the one marked 'up'.

'See you at rounds tonight,' he said in a neutral tone, then his lift arrived and he strode into it, as eager as she was, it seemed, to leave their shared, lingering awareness behind.

'I talked with John this afternoon,' reported Linda Jorgansen, tossing a strand of red hair back over her shoulder as she consulted the notes on her clipboard. 'There's a wide range of foods he's willing to try. . .'

'Whether he'll still be as willing after he's tasted the hospital version is another matter,' Eden Hartfield came in drily.

The comment broke the serious mood of the Friday evening round, which was one of the biggest, longest and most detailed of the week. Several people laughed and Hannah noticed that the red-headed dietician seemed to think it was the funniest thing she had heard in months. Wasn't the woman laying the flattery on a bit thick, there?

What a sour thought! Hannah was ashamed of it at once—and then immediately noticed that Linda Jorgansen was holding her clipboard so that Eden could see it, and positively snuggling up to him as she asked if he could read a certain word.

'It *is* veal, isn't it?' she questioned him earnestly. 'I can't read my own writing. Isn't that dreadful?'

'You should have been a doctor, then. Illegible handwriting has been a traditional requirement in our profession for centuries.'

Again the drily humorous comment—not *that* humorous!—drew immoderate laughter from Linda.

She had a pretty laugh, and she knew it. . . Oh, heavens, *stop* this!

'Hannah, do you have a problem?' Eden had seen

the frown Hannah had unconsciously worn as she scolded herself.

'No, not at all. I just wondered if Linda had asked Mrs Ewbanks yet about preparing extra meals for John at home.'

'Yes, I got a list from him of all his favourites, and rang her to suggest the ones with the highest amounts of protein and fat. I'll come in over the weekend to check on how he's been doing.'

The group of doctors, medical students and other qualified professionals such as Linda moved on to the next room. Terry MacNamara was one of the less severely burned victims of the plane crash and needed only one more graft before they could start thinking about discharge. A medical student, new to this hospital on a six-week rotation, was presenting an update on Terry's case this afternoon, and, since the man was Hannah's patient, she had to listen carefully so that she could fill in the blanks and ask some questions that would stretch the young student's knowledge.

She suppressed a sigh. Usually she enjoyed rounds, but not today. She was too aware of Eden, and was trying too hard not to be. It made the whole thing seem like hard work. Tired feet inside shoes that chafed at the heel begged for her to sit down, her arms and shoulders scolded her for wearing such a close-fitting blouse, and her head insisted with a dull rhythmic throb that the lighting in here was far too bright and harsh.

Thank goodness it was the weekend! On call for serious emergencies and committed to at least one visit to check on her own patients, she wasn't guaranteed a complete break. But *I should manage to stay away for the whole of tomorrow*, she promised herself. *And I can do anything I like with my day. . .* For the moment, this luxury was enough.

Until she found herself heading down to the ground floor in the lift with Eden Hartfield and Linda Jorgansen.

'What are your plans for the weekend, Dr Hartfield?' the dietician cooed—or it sounded like a coo to Hannah.

'Oh, it's pretty full,' the doctor replied. '*Very* full, actually. I've got a dinner and a barbecue. Friends passing through from interstate. Some gardening I promised to do for my sister-in-law. And of course a backlog of medical reading to do. I always have that.'

'My goodness!' Linda said, clearly taken aback by the full schedule and his detailed account of it. 'I was wondering if you were going to that crafts festival at Tharwa. I am. . . But obviously, you don't have a moment to spare for anything like that.'

Her laugh was a little nervous and uncertain now, as if she was afraid she had been too obvious about her interest in him.

She has! Hannah decided. And that long list of activities was just to fob her off. He's running a mile!

Then, once again, she felt bad about the moment of malicious pleasure she had taken in Linda Jorgansen's discomfort and Eden's clear lack of interest in the other woman.

Why shouldn't they get togther? She was really very nice. Just because she herself was lonely. . .

It was the first time she had let herself use the word, but she knew it was true. Canberra had never been the easiest of places to make friends. She had lost touch years ago with most of her friends from school, and those to whom she still wrote no longer lived here. Beth was in Paris. Caroline in Washington. Maureen in Western Australia. Her London friends, too, were half a world away, and in the two months since her return to her native land she had been so busy that leisure interests had been out of the question. Even her relationships with other doctors at the hospital — except Eden Hartfield — were still of the most superficial kind.

'With Gina gone, Eden is the person I know best here, now. That's ridiculous! Awful!'

She left him and Linda chatting beside the lift on the ground floor and hurried off towards the car park after the briefest of goodbyes. The dietician seemed to have recovered her poise now. Perhaps if she toned down her pursuit of Eden a little, she would have a chance with the man after all. . .

I *won't* be jealous! she told herself. Tomorrow I'll ring up the YMCA or someone. Find a course to do. Join a gym. Or a gourmet dining club.

Suddenly desperate to get away from the hospital with its load of work that could engulf her so easily, Hannah stormed through the car park, her heels clicking like those of a Spanish dancer. Bag and coat flung in the back, seatbelt on, keys in the ignition, engine started and quickly warmed.

It was a lovely evening. Big white clouds over in the west promised a spectacular sunset over the blue-etched Brindabella Ranges later on. It was staying light quite late now, and the longest day of the year was only a month and a half away. That meant summer, and swimming, and barbecues. Eden had said that he was going to one this weekend. . .

She slammed on the brakes, narrowly missing his knees with the corner of her front bumper, and stalled the engine. He had loomed in front of the car so suddenly, and, frankly, she hadn't been paying attention. Quickly she wound down the window and leaned her head out to him.

'Eden! I'm terribly sorry!'

'Do you always walk that fast?' He was frowning impatiently.

'What? I just about ran you down with my car and you're criticising the speed of my walk?'

'If you hadn't left me in the lurch like that with Linda, then scuttled across the car park like a crab in an Olympic marathon, I wouldn't have had to step out in front of your car to flag you down and it wouldn't have been a problem! I've been hallooing at you all the way from the main doors. People must think I'm crazy.'

'Well, perhaps you are.' She made the words deliberately light. He was sending pulses of awareness all through her with the untidy, slightly breathless look he wore. The top button of his shirt was undone and he wore no tie today. The shirt was that same classic blue he had worn the night he had cleaned out Sally's guttering.

'Crazy?' he echoed. 'Perhaps I am. Unlock this passenger door for me and pull over somewhere. There are three cars behind you now, trying to get out of the car park, and you're blocking their way. We can't talk here.'

'What are we talking about?'

'Just let me in, woman!'

She had to do so. The car behind her had begun to beep impatiently, and, until Eden had pointed out the fact, she hadn't even been aware that she was blocking the exit-lane. What was wrong with her tonight? If she always drove this badly she'd be a menace on the roads!

Starting the engine again, she at once stalled it as she tried to move off, and this time two cars honked before she succeeded in getting under way.

'Whatever it is you've got to say, Eden, it had better be worth hearing, because at this rate I'll never get home in one piece!' she told him when she had finally and thankfully come to a successful halt in a newly vacated parking space.

'I hope you'll think it's worth hearing,' he answered, far more seriously than she had expected. No teasing about the comment at all. 'I wanted to tell you that I was an idiot to cancel that picnic six weeks ago. Could we try the whole thing again?'

CHAPTER SEVEN

THE sun was shining, the air was a tiny bit crisp but full of the promise of perfect, balmy warmth later on, and even yesterday's clouds, which had created their glorious sunset as evening came on, had dissipated now. The sky was a yawning cavern of blue — the intense blue that only an Australian sky could ever be, Hannah thought, filled with a passionate love of the landscapes she had missed so badly so many times during her eight years in London.

The doubts she had felt yesterday about her life in Canberra had vanished, and if it was foolish to see the world so differently just because she was going on a picnic to Tidbinbilla with Eden Hartfield. . .well, then, let her be foolish for a day!

He was collecting her at ten, but they were skipping brunch this time. Somehow, she didn't have a very good feeling about croissants any more, but she did fit in a very long shower and had ample time to decide on a very casual pair of jeans, black leather walking shoes, and a short-sleeved plaid cotton blouse. Eden arrived at her front door promptly and was as casually dressed himself, his jeans faded and snug-fitting, and his khaki shirt rolled at the sleeves and open at the neck.

'Let's go!'

'We couldn't have picked a better day.'

The roads had all been changed since she was last out this way, and they drove past a mushroom-growth of new suburbs whose contours were still harsh and raw from their recent construction. Here and there lawns had been put in, and the old gum trees that

120

remained from the days when this had been sheep
pasture served as a reminder that soon new trees would
soften and beautify the landscape.

It was just as they were leaving these suburbs and
heading into the open country that beckoned them
towards the southern ranges of the Brindabellas when
Eden suddenly swore under his breath and picked up
the phone. 'Damn! I'm sorry, but I must ring Sally.
She left a message on my machine while I was in the
shower this morning and I completely forgot to return
it.'

He dialled and waited, leaving a tiny tension to fill
the silence. Hannah had wanted to avoid the subject of
Steve, Gina and Sally today; had been utterly *determined* to avoid it, in fact, since it was the thing that
seemed unfailingly to create problems between herself
and Eden. . . And now here it was already, coming up
like an unexpected cloud on the horizon and casting its
familiar shadow.

'Sally?' Eden said. 'Yes, hi. . . No, I was in the
shower. . .the car-phone, yes. I'm probably between
transmitting cells if it sounds crackly and faint. . .
Dinner tonight?' He looked across at Hannah and
hesitated. 'Actually, I'd decided to do the garden for
you tomorrow instead, if that's all right.' He listened
for a while. 'No, of course I don't mind. If you've got
the chance of a break from the boys all day tomorrow,
and to have a friend over to lunch. . . Late this
afternoon, then. Bye.'

He hung up, but said nothing to Hannah and she was
immediately absorbed in coping with an absurd disappointment. She had been hoping that this picnic would
flow on into dinner together, and now he had promised
to work on his sister-in-law's garden later today.

Then she remembered what he had said to Linda
Jorgansen yesterday afternoon in the lift and blurted

accusingly, 'Don't you have dinner and a barbecue and friends and all sorts of things this weekend? I've just remembered! And now the gardening and dinner as well. Why didn't you leave yourself some breathing space? We could have done this next weekend just as well.'

'There's no barbecue and no friends passing through,' he confessed, turning towards her with a shrug. His mouth twisted. 'I made all that up for Linda's benefit. As for dinner. . . I was hoping to have that with you.'

'Oh. . .' She flushed with pleasure and the cloud on the horizon vanished as quickly as it had come.

'But I couldn't say no to Sally. She hates asking me to do work around the place for her, but there really is no one else and it would be disastrous if she let the place fall into disrepair and lowered its value. I imagine that —— ' he hesitated, then went on firmly ' — if there's a divorce, she'll sell the place and buy something cheaper and smaller, you see. So when she tries to pay me in kind for the work I do, by feeding me home-cooked meals —— '

'Rightly guessing that you don't eat nearly as well as you should most of the time,' Hannah came in severely.

'Exactly. And the more she can do for me in that line, the more she'll let me do for her. So I always try to accept her invitations. Even when it's awkward. Like tonight.'

He reached across and brushed fingers along her bare forearm in a light caress that had her melting instantly. The sound of the phone broke the moment. It was Sally again. He listened for a moment then said carefully, 'Yes, it *is* Hannah. . . I'll ask her.'

Muffling the receiver with his thigh so that he could still use his other hand to drive, Eden said, 'She's inviting you to dinner as well.'

'Oh. . .'

'You don't have to accept.'

'All right, then, I won't,' she aswered quickly.

'Look, it's all right if you *do* come. . .'

'Do. . .do you want me to, or ——'

'I want you to, Hannah,' he said with quiet emphasis. A very short exchange, but somehow they both knew it was important.

'Then I will,' she told him breathlessly, and he picked up the phone again.

Nothing more was said about the conversation, but it was there between them all the same, like a pact they had made to go forward together with confidence. This was *their* relationship now, and, for today, at least, it couldn't be spoiled by thoughts of anyone else.

'Too early for lunch,' Eden said, as they cruised through the entrance gates to the park and began to head up the valley that led to the dreaming, forested mountain slopes where hiking trails ran through cool, moist gullies. 'What do you think? Animals first, then lunch, then our hike?'

'Sounds good.'

They didn't stop at the Visitors' Centre, although it always had interesting displays. Hannah's urge to be outdoors was too strong. The air was tangy with the scent of eucalyptus, and birds hidden deep in the trees gave off calls of a sweet, piping clarity that Hannah had never heard in other parts of the world.

The place was busy today, of course. On a glorious Saturday in late spring, everyone had the same fever in their blood. But the animal enclosures were each acres in size and Hannah was still able to feel a zesty sense of adventure and solitude as she crunched along rough pathways or struck off across the grass with Eden in search of kangaroos.

The wallabies and euros were shy today, but when

they reached the more open enclosure where the big reds were kept, and searched the tree shadows that were growing ever shorter on the grass as the sun climbed, they found what Hannah wanted to see.

'Oh, yes!' she exclaimed softly to the slowly lolloping creature. Grey. A female, then. Only the males had that soft, sandy-red hue to their fur. '*Do* come here. Do come.'

She held her fingers out very slowly and moved towards the creature, careful not to make any sudden movements or to rush her progress at all. The kangaroo lolloped forward again, bent her head and crunched on some grass, but she was wary, and didn't really want to eat. Curious, too. 'And look, you've got a joey,' Hannah crooned. 'Please let us see him!'

And in the end, after several more long moments of careful movement, they did. The head of a well-grown joey appeared, the mother relaxed. . .'Although how anyone could look as contented and comfortable as she does with her pouch full of a heavy monster like that, I don't know,' Hannah whispered to Eden. 'Look, it's practically dragging the ground!' And they were able to touch her fur.

It surprised Hannah, as it always did, with its softness. The bush was so scrubby and prickly and the soil often so hard and rocky out on the western plains where these creatures lived, you expected their fur to be coarse like pig or horse hair, but it wasn't.

The mother only put up with being patted for a moment, then suddenly she was off, the weight of the joey slowing her down so that soon she stopped and the small one, almost as if she had turfed him out, tumbled on to powerful, gangly legs and hopped away on his own just ahead of her.

Hannah laughed delightedly. 'Isn't that a sight? As a child I used to crave one as a pet. You know, the whole bit—feeding it out of a bottle, having it sleep in my bed—but now I can only think of what it would do to the lawn.'

'Not to mention the furniture! Those claws are powerful when it wants them to be.'

'Listen to our priorities! Furniture? Lawn? What do those things matter against the chance of having a *pet kangaroo*.' She gave the words an intonation that suggested that of an anguished ten-year-old. 'No wonder kids sometimes think adults have no sense of proportion at all!'

They laughed and walked on, finding other enclosures containing emus and water-birds and ending up back at the car with a zesty appetite for lunch. Eden had provided vast amounts of it. They each made themselves sandwiches of outrageous size, cramming the long, crusty French sticks with salad, ham and avocado, and wolfing them down in minutes.

'What will you think if I have another one, I wonder?' Eden mused aloud, leaning back on his hands as they sat on the picnic rug together beneath dappled shade.

'I'll think, thank goodness, that means I can do the same! Because the rest of that loaf is beckoning and I haven't even tried the pâté or the cheese yet. And I'm sure they'd both go perfectly with this wine.' She raised the plastic picnic glass that was moulded into the shape of an elegant wine goblet, and ice cubes bobbed about in the light, dry liquid.

'Save room for dessert,' Eden advised a few minutes later as he saw her second sandwich being piled as high as the first. His own was, if anything, higher.

'Dessert? I couldn't!'

'Then let's pack it in this day-pack along with the Thermos and have tea and French pastries on a mossy rock somewhere halfway through our hike.'

Hannah could only groan in disbelief. . .and blissful
anticipation. She finished sandwich and wine, then
found that somehow she was stretching out like a sleepy
cat on the rug and closing her eyes. This cotton
sweatshirt, which she didn't need to wear as it was now
so delightfully warm, made an extremely comfortable
pillow, and the gurgling water rushing over rounded
pebbles in the nearby creek was as melodious as a
lullaby. . .

At first, that incredibly soft nuzzling against her lips
was part of a marvellous dream about floating. . .or
swimming. . .and feathers. . .and a big. . .something.
She didn't know what. The image was fading, and she
was waking up but she didn't want to, in case that
made this kissing stop.

Kissing? 'I thought if I kissed you, you'd wake up,'
came a murmuring voice. 'But obviously you need
sterner tactics. What sterner tactics do I know, though?
Somehow I've forgotten. . .'

'It doesn't matter,' she mumbled against his mouth.
'I don't need stern tactics. I don't need to wake up at
all. Can't we just stay like this. . .?'

'I'd love to, but there's an emu just behind your
shoulder who's getting curious and I think he's about
to try and steal the remains of our lunch.'

'Aark!' She sat up, her head still swimming with
drowsiness. There was an emu eyeing them with its
large, brown and very inhuman-looking eyes, but it
was safe at a distance of several metres and Hannah
pelted Eden with an empty paper bag. 'You cruel
man!' The creature stalked off, the untidy mound of
brown-grey feathers over its back bouncing like a grass
skirt.

'Should I have let you sleep? If we want to fit in a
hike *and* look for koalas afterwards. . .'

'Yes, you're right. I'll go and splash my face with

creek water. That wine was delightful, but a mistake in the middle of the day.'

'Splash your face,' he approved. 'But first. . .'

He placed firm fingers on her shoulders then slid them upwards across her collarbone and throat so that they framed her face as he touched her lips again. He didn't linger there, just plucked the kiss from her like taking the stone from a ripe cherry, but she knew that the brief touch was a promise of things to come and she gave herself to it freely. It was startling how easily her body responded to him, the warmth of the sun on her clothing mingling with a stronger inner warmth to produce quicksilver fire all through her.

'I'll splash my face,' she gasped, and fled to the creek, aware that there were other picnickers nearby. Surely they could see the dark flush on her face from metres away!

The water was still as cold as snow-melt and, she hoped as she cupped her hands together, pure enough to drink. The icy freshness on her cheeks and sliding down her throat served finally to wash away the sleepy, sensual, cat-like feeling, and when she returned to Eden and helped him to pack up rug, picnic basket and left-overs, she was able to smile and chat easily.

They drove up a side road to another car park from which the hiking trails began, and chose one of medium length that would wind around a secretive little creek and then climb higher to slightly drier, more open forest. The printed sign told them that lyre-birds could sometimes be seen and heard along this track.

'Although since they can mimic every other bird in the bush and even the sound of an axe chopping wood, so I've heard, I don't know how we'd realise that it was a lyre-bird we were hearing,' Eden said.

'And they're supposed to be shy, too, aren't they?'

'I think so, yes.'

He shouldered the day-pack and led the way, with Hannah following closely behind. They could have talked, but they chose not to. Silence was nicer, enabling them to hear every nuance of the bush sounds — the rustle of leaves, the hidden gurgle of water, the drowsy drone of a fly and the call of birds.

Hannah even tried to make her footfalls softer for a while, choosing a damp patch of ground or a firm rock to step on instead of a crunching twig or a torn, brittle piece of bark. . .but she had to admit to herself that she was hopeless at this. No self-respecting lyre-bird would remain within a mile of her thumping shoes, and after a while she decided to enjoy the rhythmic tramping for its own sake and forget about serious bird-watching.

At the highest point of the trail they stopped and found the mossy rock that Eden had promised her.

'I didn't believe it when you said we'd enjoy our tea and cakes here,' she told him. 'But I will. I'm hungry again!'

'It's the open air,' he said. 'If only we could bring some of our burn patients out here. They'd soon down those daily calories.'

It was the first time today that they had talked about work, and by unworded consent they let the subject lapse again at once. It was always too easy to think about patients, treatments, bureaucratic business.

'This tea tastes good,' Hannah said instead. 'I'm thirstier than I thought.'

'There's enough hot water for another cup.'

'No, thanks.' She shivered suddenly. 'Mm, we're in shade and I've cooled down. The shadows are lengthening.'

'Don't get cold.'

He shifted towards her on the moss and squeezed her against him with an arm that was strong and heavy and still very warm. No other hikers were in sight, and they turned their faces together at the same time, their kiss the culmination of the perfect day. His throat and temples were faintly dewy with sweat, but the mild, masculine scent of it, mingled with his aftershave and the smell of the bush, only stirred her more powerfully.

Pressed against him, she could feel the rise and fall of his breathing, the tickle of his hair and the tingling sensitivity of her own breasts that seemed suddenly strained and tight against the lacy cups of her bra and the cotton of her shirt. When he moved his hands to explore the weight of the twin globes she arched upwards and felt his breath cool the dewy moisture at her throat, although the rest of her was on fire again.

'Eden. . .'

'Hannah. . . Oh, lord, it's good to get away here where nothing else matters, isn't it?' he murmured throatily. 'Today this is nobody's business but our own. . .'

A rustle and a crack in the undergrowth nearby startled them into springing apart, and Hannah scraped her thigh uncomfortably on the rock. She looked up, embarrassed, expecting to see a party of hikers staring at them with ill-concealed grins. Three buttons of his shirt were undone. . .and two buttons of her own blouse, so that it fell open to show two edges of pale blue cotton lace and two swelling slopes of flesh.

But there were no hikers. Instead, she barely glimpsed the golden-brown shape of the bird, its lyre-shaped tail not raised in display, as it always was in nature photographs, but smoothed down towards the ground as it scuttled off into the bush again.

'Look, Eden, it's a ——'

The creature had disappeared again before she even had time to finish the sentence.

Eden was laughing. 'We were looking for a lyre-bird at every step and now. . .'

'Just when we weren't in the least bit interested,' she came in, laughing as well.

'. . .the audacious creature comes and crashes our private party.'

'He didn't stay long.'

'Perhaps he didn't like the music.'

'What music?'

'Oh. . .bells? Trumpets? Sky-rockets and cannons? Or maybe flutes and violins, very soft and very sweet,' he finished in a low tone, then reached towards her and very carefully buttoned her blouse. The brush of his fingers against her breasts was soft and teasing, and the breath caught in her throat as she waited for him to finish, unable to move at all. 'We have to get back,' he whispered, then went on in a more practical tone, 'And I think we might have to skip the koalas. Sally is expecting us in time for me to be of some use in the garden, and it's a big lawn to mow.'

'The afternoon seems to have dropped through a hole in the ground,' Hannah managed, hiding her disappointment. 'I would have said it wasn't even three yet, but by the sun and those shadows. . .'

'Closer to four, I'd say,' he agreed, scrambling off the rock on to his feet and shouldering the day-pack once again.

The movement opened the unbuttoned shirt across his chest, revealing the hard, square shapes of his muscles, their contours blurred by a regular pattern of dark hair. Hannah ached to do as he had done for her — to go up to him, stand very close, and fasten those three buttons, but somehow their talk of time and of getting to Sally's had broken the mood and she didn't dare. In the end, he left the shirt as it was.

Maybe he was glad of the air cooling his skin. Maybe he just hadn't noticed.

The last half of the track didn't seem long at all. It was mostly downhill, and Eden was setting a faster pace this time. Still, it was half-past four when they arrived at the car, and it was cool and shaded there now, instead of swimming in dappled sunlight as it had been when they left it. Eden dived into a black sweatshirt and Hannah followed his lead, finding the cream one that had pillowed her head on the rug after lunch.

The koalas were out of the question, she knew, and they didn't even dally long enough for her to grab another drink of the biting cold mountain creek water.

'I hate letting her down,' Eden said, after driving in silence at the very edge of the speed limit for ten minutes. 'I told her no later than four-thirty. She was hoping I'd have time to dig out the worst of the weeds in the front shrubbery—some of those thistles look about eight feet high—but there won't be time for that now. We'll eat early because of the boys, and after that it will be dark.'

'I can do the weeds,' Hannah offered.

'She won't let you. . .and neither will I.'

'Why ever not!'

'Because it's not your problem. Best if you don't get involved.'

She fumed in silence, both angry and upset. The blunt words had closed a door in her face, or drawn a line at her feet which she was not to go beyond. It reminded her of the signs at the hospital that read, 'Authorised Personnel Only Beyond This Point'.

He let me help at Sally's the night of the flood because he had to, she realised. But now he's excluding me, and I don't know why. Perhaps he wishes now that I wasn't coming to Sally's at all. Is it still because I'm

Gina's sister? I'm in the other camp? Or does he have his own reasons for keeping this thing casual, with no shared responsibility for each other's lives and problems?

They arrived at Sally's without another word being spoken.

'You weren't worried, I hope,' Eden said to his sister-in-law at once. 'Our hike took longer than we expected.'

'I guessed as much,' she reassured him. 'It was such a glorious day. Still is!'

'I'll do the lawn straight away.'

'I've put petrol in the mower for you already.'

'You shouldn't have,' he scolded, his eye travelling instinctively, as Hannah's did, to the growing round-ness at her waist.

'Well, I did! I'm not completely helpless, you know!' Sally retorted with spirit.

Eden disappeared out the back and Hannah asked as soon as he was out of earshot, 'What about me? Eden said you had some weeding. . .'

'Heavens, no! But if you wouldn't mind. . . It would be such a treat to do dinner without the boys under my feet and dinning in my ears. Could you take them into the back garden and play with them?'

'Of course!'

'Try the sand-pit. They love that. Or the swings. And keep them out of range of that mower. It has been known to shoot a piece of gravel up every now and then, if one gets caught beneath the wheels.'

She turned to the boys, who were indeed very much under her feet in the kitchen — very noisy, too — and said, 'Go outside with Dr. . .?' She gave Hannah a questioning look.

'Just Hannah,' she came in quickly.

But Sally grimaced. 'If you don't mind,' she said in

an apologetic aside, 'I'd prefer the formal title. I'm old-fashioned, I know, but I want my kids to respect adults, and I think it helps if they *don't* call everyone they meet by Christian names straight away.'

'Well, it's Lombard. Hannah Lombard,' Hannah blurted awkwardly. What else could she do?

'Dr Lombard,' Sally nodded. She had flinched visibly, but covered it quickly with a smile, and Hannah pretended not to notice. Sally didn't realise, of course, that Eden's new friend knew exactly why the name Lombard was a difficult one for her. And clearly the family resemblance between Hannah and Gina was too slight to create any suspicion that they might be related. 'Boys, go outside with Dr Lombard and show her your swings and slippery-dip. . . Oh, these onions! They seem extra stinging today!'

She wiped away tears which probably *were* caused by the half-chopped onion on the kitchen bench in front of her, and Hannah quickly stepped in to say to the children, 'Have you got your very own slippery-dip? Can I have a slide on it?'

The idea of a staid adult, and a doctor, what was more, doing such a childish thing captured their attention at once and even little Geoffrey, who could be very clingy, was eager to rush out and witness the spectacle. Sally threw Hannah a grateful look as two pairs of small feet made an impossible clatter through the back passage. 'Thanks! If Eden lets *you* get away, he's crazy!'

Hannah laughed, blushed and escaped outside. She did enough sliding to satisfy two giggling boys then sat on a garden bench and watched them in the sand-pit, suggesting new games whenever their interest flagged, and mediating in the small disputes that threatened frequently, due to little Geoffrey's utter disregard for Ben's carefully constructed castles and roads.

Both boys were clearly active and intelligent. . .and exhausting! She thought of Sean Carroll still lying in his special bed in the burns unit. Just a few minutes of less vigilant supervision by his mother had meant weeks of pain and difficulty for the little boy, and anguish for both parents.

No wonder Sally felt overwhelmed! How did she ever get anything done at all? Hannah wondered.

Still, there *were* moments of peace, and in them she shamelessly watched Eden. The power-mower was an old one and performed about as graciously as a pension-aged horse in a bad riding school. It seemed to know exactly the worst moment at which to stall, balked at any sugestion of a tough weed or an overlong tussock of grass, and protested with whines and roars if there was anything other than soft, smooth soil and fine grass beneath its blades.

Four times Hannah saw Eden wrenching at the pull-starter, having to use all his strength to get the thing going again. Three times he had to detach the bin that caught the cut grass and carry it over to dump its contents on to a run-down compost pile.

Dampness darkened his shirt now in places that had been quite dry during even the most strenuous parts of their hike this afternoon. When he had finished the back garden, he let the loud, raucous machine remain blessedly silent for a few minutes and came over to Hannah.

'I need to start doing this every week now, instead of every fortnight. The mower can't handle grass this long, and it's growing faster in the warmer weather.'

'What you need,' she retorted, 'is a new mower! I've heard they actually make models these days that you can operate without doing a six-month body-building course and three months of motor mechanics beforehand!'

'Do you think I don't know it? I've offered to buy her one but she won't let me.'

'And look what her stubbornness is costing you! A new mower would do this job twice as fast with half the trouble. Tell her it's inconsiderate of her to be so proud on this issue.'

'No. . .'

'*I'll* tell her, then!'

'Don't.'

'Why? Because it's not my problem?'

'If you want to put it like that, yes.'

'*You* put it like that yourself earlier. What are you telling me, Eden? That I'm not part of your life? That this is something very casual we've got going here? OK, fine! I'll accept that, but I think you could have found a more tactful way to get it across!'

They glared at each other. Around them, the late afternoon air was redolent with the smell of newly cut grass. Eden had grass stains on his hands and a smear of motor oil across his face. His sweatshirt had been flung on to the back porch long ago and those three buttons on the khaki shirt beneath were still undone, showing that even the dark hair on his chest was a little dampened by sweat. And, in spite of her anger, Hannah's whole body ached to touch him, taste him, taste even the grass and the sweat.

'We can't talk about this now, damn it!' he growled. The boys were absorbed in amicable play for the moment, just a few metres away, but there was no telling how long that might last. He swore impatiently under his breath and went on abruptly, 'But. . .*casual*? Given the awkward situation involving our respective siblings, do you think I'd be bothering with it at all if it was something unimportant? This *isn't* a casual thing! Not as far as I'm concerned.' The blue intensity of his gaze left her in no doubt about his sincerity.

'Me neither,' she admitted in a low breathless voice.

'Then what are we saying? What does that mean?'

'That you let me help you, and let me start to be friends with Sally.'

'It's not as simple as that, Hannah,' he told her heavily.

'Dinner's ready, everyone,' Sally called from the back door at that moment.

CHAPTER EIGHT

'DON'T stay while I put the boys to bed,' Sally told
Hannah and Eden after the delicious meal of home-
made vegetable soup, spaghetti and salad had been
eaten, and the kitchen cleaned up. 'Because by the
time that's done, I'll be ready for bed myself and
I won't be good company if I stay up. Sorry, but
Geoffrey's always up by six and Ben's been waking in
the night a lot lately, since Steve left.'

'You don't have to apologise, Sally,' Eden growled.
'I'm only sorry I didn't get round to the front lawn.'

'Half of it's dead out the front anyway,' Sally laughed
helplessly. 'It gets too much leaf and bark litter from
the big gum trees. I've been wanting to put in some
native Australian shrubs and flowers there, lots of
spiky, spidery red things like bottle-brush and grevillea,
but I guess that'll have to be up to the next people.'

'The next people?'

'I might as well be realistic, Eden. If there's a
divorce, we'll sell the house. This Gina creature—
sorry, I can't speak about her in a civil tone!—is only
in her twenties, I gather. She'll want children of her
own eventually, and a decent house to bring them up
in. Can you imagine Steve supporting two full house-
holds when he's barely managing as it is? Or me
meeting the mortgage payments here on my own if I
go back to work?'

It was only what Eden himself had already said to
Hannah privately, but it had an added sting when
coming from Sally in that tone that tried to be brisk,

cheerful and matter-of-fact but didn't quite manage it. Hannah had flushed at the sound of her sister's name.

If she *weren't* my sister, I'd be up in arms on Sally's behalf, she realised. Just as Eden is.

A few minutes later Eden was driving her home and she knew that the silence between them was because each was still mulling over the issue. He was the one to break it.

'When are we going to tell her?'

'That I'm the Gina creature's sister?' The attempt at flippancy didn't work.

He frowned. 'Yes.'

'I don't know.' She wanted to add pleadingly, Let's not think about it now. Let's keep this all in the present. But she didn't.

'That conference is only a month away, you know.'

'What conference?' It seemed like a strange leap from the talk about Sally.

'The international conference on trauma management up in Queensland. You don't mean. . .? My God, in all the kerfuffle over the plane crash and our extra load have we never discussed it?'

'Unless I've developed some sort of selective amnesia. . .' Then she suddenly remembered their receptionist, Annette Kenyon's cryptic reference over two months ago to Dr Hartfield's 'going to Queensland in December,' and the last small mystery about that initial confusion of identity was cleared away. She had forgotten all about it.

'I'd better tell you now, then, since Bruce wants us both to go,' Eden was saying. 'He'll bring someone down from Sydney with him to help cover the workload while we're away. Most of the sessions will be very important and useful from our perspective. Peter Harrison and Alan James from the Accident and

Emergency trauma team will be going, too. It's a four-day affair ——'

'Including time off for golf?'

'That, too,' he agreed drily, recognising as she did that these things were never all work and no play. 'And it's being held at a very plush convention centre on the Gold Coast.'

'But that's only an hour's drive from where Gina and Steve are ——'

'I know. That's why I brought it up. I'm going to go and see him. Maybe even stay for an extra night. I think I can manage to skip the golf.'

'And what do you hope to achieve?' she queried a little coolly. His tone had been ominous, ruthless, and his face had set into hard planes.

But now he sighed and the shade of ruthlessness was gone. 'I don't know. Perhaps, like you, I just want to understand their side of it.'

'I can see, now, why Sally's side is always uppermost in your mind,' she told him quietly.

'And with each day that passes, you and I are caught more firmly in the middle.'

By unworded consent, they let the subject lapse during the last few minutes of the drive to her house, each wanting to regain the mood of today's picnic. When he pulled up in her driveway, she asked him, with a catch of nervousness in her throat, 'Would you like to come in for some tea or coffee? It's still very early. Only nine. . .'

'Glad you asked,' he drawled. 'I'd like to come in very much.'

It was midnight before he left, and coffee had given way to a late-night snack improvised with much laughter in the kitchen. Ice-cream, crushed nuts, chocolate sauce and a garnish of liqueur cherries that were far too potent to be consumed on their own—this last item being a recent gift from a patient.

Hannah had put on some mellow jazz music and it had formed such an unobtrusive background to their talking that she hadn't even noticed when it finished. She had found out a lot more about Eden Hartfield tonight: that he collected antique marbles and played squash twice a week; that his father had died some years ago and his mother was remarried and living in Tasmania; that he was allergic to pineapple and loved cashew nuts. . .and that he had deliberately avoided any serious involvement with a woman all during his training, but now he knew he was ready to put that side of his life first. . .

'Although I do plan on being at the hospital at six-thirty tomorrow morning to check on my patients,' he had finished with deliberate flippancy. 'Which I suppose is a sign that I'll never be able to be as selfish as I want to be.'

'Don't forget that there are such things as interns and junior residents on call,' she had reminded him teasingly.

'So you're saying that we'll be able to take some time off in the future if we really need it?'

'I hope so. . .'

Till now, tonight, he hadn't kissed her, but a kiss had been in the air between them with every word they spoke. Now, they both knew that the moment was right. It wasn't a difficult transition. They had been sitting on the same couch, the soft teal-blue fabric-covered cushions doing everything they could to coax the pair into a comfortable slouch. With ice-cream finished and glass bowls set on the coffee table, out of the way, they could move across the small space that separated them with scarcely any effort at all.

She knew the taste and feel of his lips now—warm,

firm, smooth and sweetly flavoured tonight with ice-cream and cherry liqueur — but if anything this familiarity only made the ache deep inside her more insistent in its painful, pleasurable throbbing. After that first hot, full touch, he brushed his mouth away, leaving her bereft and hungry for him at once, but then, before she had time to moan in protest at the deprivation, he had pulled her weight on to him so that she felt the rise and fall of his breathing as it massaged the softness of her breasts.

When his hands sought to explore the creamy skin beneath her blouse and slipped open the fastening of her bra, she did not protest but lost herself in the silky magic of his touch. She found a pleasure just as intense in discovering the texture of his skin, too — the roughness of his jaw that would need shaving again within a few hours, the more tender skin at the corners of his eyes that betrayed a fine tracery of lines in strong light, the hard, straight bridge of his nose where a grease streak from the old lawn-mower still showed faintly, despite his efforts before dinner to scrub it off. Lower down there was his chest, with that frankly masculine pattern of hair tapering to a silky line lower still where it disappeared into his jeans.

She did not know how long they stayed like this. It felt like hours. . .or perhaps only seconds, and it could easily have trespassed into an ultimate fulfilment that she had only known in the past, and so disastrously, with Patrick Lacey.

And it was this name, impinging on the pure sensuality of the night, that told her she had to stop this before it did reach that point of total surrender.

I'm not ready, she knew. I can't risk being hurt like that again. I'm so close to loving Eden. I don't dare to do something that will topple me over the brink without really knowing what this is all going to mean.

He seemed to sense the change in her response to him before she even knew she had made one. His fingers slowed, softened, began to unfasten the knots of ecstasy that they had been gently tying on her skin and deep within her. His breathing, which had been rhythmic and quickened and close to abandonment, became controlled, and she could feel the restraint in it. Her own hands slid away and began to fiddle with a loose thread on the back of the couch as she sat up.

'I should go home, shouldn't I?' he said in a low, throaty voice.

'Yes,' she blurted. 'You should. I don't want you to, but you should. You must.'

'Just give me a minute.'

'Of course. I'm not pushing you out of the door.'

'I want to do this again,' he said, then added hastily, 'Well, not this, but — damn! Yes! This! But you know what I mean, don't you? The whole day. And dinner. By ourselves this time.'

'Yes.'

'My place. Your place. The art gallery. A movie. Another picnic, another hike. . .'

'Yes.'

'But for now. . .'

Neither of them spoke. There was no need. And after a moment he rose to go. Longing to melt against him once more, she shivered as he trailed his fingers down her bare arm. She opened the front door for him and felt the brief feathering against her lips that was his goodnight kiss.

'You going in tomorrow?' he whispered.

'To see a few people, yes. Not as early as you.'

'In that case. . .till Monday, then.'

'Till Monday.'

And he was gone, striding down the front path as if he needed the rapid pace to shake off feelings and needs that were still too urgent and demanding. Hannah waited until he had started the car, watching and listening as he idled it for a minute to warm the engine. The night had chilled now after the warm, sunny day, and there might even be a touch of light, unseasonable frost towards morning. Standing here, in the open doorway, she was cold, but couldn't bear to tear herself away and go inside until he had really gone.

He must have seen her there, because just as he moved off he wound down the window a little and she saw his hand—just a pale shape in the darkness—curving in a wave. Raising her own hand in reply, she turned and closed the door behind her, then clutched her arms across the front of her body, giving way to the cold. The house still held warmth from the day's sun, but it was dissipating now.

Time for bed. Alone. Much the best and wisest thing, she knew, but she still ached for him all the same.

'Am I a fool to be letting myself feel like this, and so soon?' she wondered, and didn't know the answer.

'I don't like the look of this one,' Eden said to Hannah in an undertone as they stood together by the bed of the new admission, who lay there inert and mercifully oblivious to pain as most of his burns went deeper than the nerve-endings.

'I don't either.' She glanced at the monitor, whose red figures gave constant read-outs for heart-rate, blood pressure, pulmonary artery flow and central venous pressure, and at the tubing that seemed to snake around the patient like equipment in some bizarre whisky distillery: catheters; intravenous line; drainage tubes; tracheostomy. 'He's got full-thickness burns to nearly eighty per cent of his body, and, from the notes we've got here, it doesn't seem as if he was in good condition to start with. I'm afraid. . .we're going to lose him. What's the story?'

'That's what I don't like.'

'What? I —'

'The story. Is that girlfriend of his still about?'

'She was waiting outside when I came through.'

'I'd like you to talk to her, go through the drill again.'

'You mean. . .?'

'I don't think she's telling the truth about what happened. Getting ready to pour some petrol into his car, she said, but, according to the ambulance officers, that car was derelict and hadn't been driven anywhere for months. All its tyres were down. Let's see if what she tells you is consistent.'

Hannah shivered. 'You mean she's hiding something. This wasn't an accident?'

'I don't think so.'

'But surely. . . Not a suicide attempt?'

'No. Look at his left arm here, that area of unburned skin near the inner curve of the elbow.'

'Needle marks.

'Yes. I saw some of this in Detroit. More than I wanted to see. Crimes related to drug empires. Canberra doesn't have much of it, thank goodness, but it does have some, and it can get very nasty.'

'Yes; I came across some drug-related problems in London, but nothing like this. What's going on?'

'Somebody like our friend here deals in the hard stuff but is a user as well and consumes the profits. Can't pay the higher-ups what he owes them. Or tries to cheat or con them in some way. These people are ruthless when it comes to setting an example. They want their dealers to know that cheating doesn't pay. Pouring petrol over someone and setting a match to them is a fairly graphic way to show that, don't you think?' he concluded grimly.

Hannah shuddered again. 'And the girlfriend is too suspicious of the police to risk having them involved, so she's lied. . .'

'Even though it means that the people who did this to her boyfriend will get away with it,' he finished for her. 'They won't, of course. If you can confirm that her story is false. . . In fact, even now I think we've got enough to go on. We're legally obliged to report anything suspicious like this to the police within twenty-four hours.'

'Twenty-four hours. . .'

'Yes. He may not live that long.'

'Was he living before?' Hannah asked in a hard voice. 'Look at his heel. Aren't those needle marks, too? He must have been a pretty heavy user. I don't call that living, I'm afraid. . .'

'Go out and talk to the girlfriend. I want to check on a few things here, see what more we can do for him. . . although I think it's just a matter of time.'

Hannah left the unit and went out to the waiting area in the foyer. It was a quiet time of the evening, about eight o'clock. She and Eden had each been called in from home to see this new patient, who had been admitted about an hour before. Most of their other patients had visitors with them, getting ready to leave again, and Hannah did not expect to find many people ensconced in the low chairs.

She did expect to find one person, though — the girlfriend that Eden had talked to not long ago and who was supposed to be waiting here. She *wasn't* waiting. Hannah herself waited for several minutes, checked the bathrooms, even went down to the ground floor and looked in the foyer and the cafeteria there. The latter was nearly deserted, and no one there even remotely fitted the image she had formed of the unknown young woman.

'She's done a bunk,' Hannah reported to Eden back in the unit.

He grimaced. 'I'm not completely surprised. She was obviously nervous and uncomfortable about even being here. At the time I put it down to her concern over Damien here, but——'

'We've got her name, haven't we? She may need help herself. Legal help. Grief counselling. Help in getting away from the drug scene. . .'

'Yes, we have her name, and the address of course. Here. . .' He looked down at the new patient's chart. 'Buffy Delaney.'

'What?'

'Buffy Delaney. Sounds like a——'

'Eden, that's not a name.' Hannah sighed. 'I guess the people who admitted him and took down all these details were all male. . .or at least not very interested in fashion.'

'I don't get it.'

'Buffy Delaney is the name of a very exclusive women's clothing boutique in the city centre.'

'Then this girl definitely doesn't want to be involved. I don't think we need any more evidence, here. I'm going to call the police.'

Two police officers had arrived within minutes to interview Hannah, Eden and the ambulance officers who had brought in the critically injured man. Their questions, particularly to Eden, were detailed, and when they left it was in order to go to the house in the suburb of Narrabundah where Damien Fielder and his girlfriend had been living.

'We might as well go home,' Eden said to Hannah soon afterwards. 'There's nothing more we can do.'

Their patient died during the night, and everyone

who had seen him agreed that it was for the best. The police had found his house deserted and no further word had been heard from 'Buffy Delaney'. The drug user's next of kin was listed as an uncle with a post-office address in a country town several hundred miles away, and efforts were begun immediately to contact him.

It was a sad and very grim story, and even though their other patients had not been told about it, some of the details leaked out and lowered morale throughout the unit. Hannah was glad that she had surgery that morning, and didn't look forward to going up to the seventh floor again later in the day to see her patients.

It was four days since her picnic with Eden, and she wished that the mood in the burns unit could reflect her own happiness. They hadn't spent any time together since Saturday, but he had suggested the art gallery, a movie and dinner this coming weekend, and she was already looking forward to it with a giddy pleasure that occasionally frightened her but mostly made her tread around the hospital very lightly.

I feel so lucky this week, she thought to herself on Wednesday afternoon as she went up to the burns unit after lunch. Why can't everyone have a small piece of my happiness and good fortune?

First she checked on Sean, who had had the last of his skin grafts done by Eden that morning. He was still groggy from anaesthesia, and the places where a healthy layer of skin had been removed to donate to a more deeply injured section were now themselves raw and painful. They would heal quickly, however.

Helen Carroll was there, watching the little boy's face intently and holding his hand. As she turned to greet Hannah, she brushed away a tear and the latter said quickly, 'I can come back later.'

'No, I'm fine,' the other woman sniffed. 'It's silly! Today I'm actually crying because I'm happy.'

'You are?'

'Yes! I've still got my little boy, and that's all that matters. I realise that now, although I didn't at first. And more than that, he'll be home in a week or two, and you say that even the worst of the scarring can be treated surgically later on. When I think of what *could* have happened. If it had been fire instead of hot water. If he'd been trapped under the flow of it for longer. If it had burnt his face. And I'm so grateful to all of you for all you've done.'

'Please. . . I always wish we could do more. Or do it faster.'

But the conversation did Hannah good, and she smiled at Gretchen Older on her way past Joan Tate's room. Joan was technically Eden's patient, but Hannah stopped in the doorway all the same to ask Gretchen, 'How is she? Her colour's a little better.'

'She's better all over,' Sister Older answered, as she attached a new bag of intravenous nutrition. 'We're definitely not going to lose her now. The kidney function is starting to return and Dr Hartfield and Dr Bliss from Renal think we should be able to wean her off dialysis quite soon. Her husband comes in and reads poetry to her every evening. He's so gallant, and he has such a wonderful reading voice. I hope *I* have a man who can be that romantic about me when I'm sixty-two!'

'I'll settle for it at forty-two!' Hannah returned, and both women laughed. Even Joan, who appeared to be fast asleep, gave a faint smile as if she knew how lucky she was to have her Gordon.

Hannah's day was brightened a little more by the encounter. Now it was time to check on John Ewbanks. He was going down for surgery on the injured side of his face tomorrow, and she wanted a last chance to gather her thoughts about how best to proceed.

But John wasn't yet ready to submit in silence to her careful examination. Since his return to a state of alertness last Friday, he had had some difficult times and had become much more demanding, ready with a barrage of questions each time a doctor saw him and sometimes appearing suspicious of the answers.

Today he wanted to know, 'That guy they brought in last night died on you, didn't he?'

'He was critically ill,' Hannah admitted. 'From the beginning, we had little hope of saving him.'

'Worse than I was at the beginning?'

'Far worse. And he didn't have your constitution and general level of fitness and health to back him up.'

'There's something pretty bizarre about the whole thing, isn't there? I heard the police were involved.'

'Don't tire yourself by wondering over it,' Hannah responded cautiously.

'You mean, don't ask any more questions because it's none of my business?' He grinned to soften the words.

'Yes, I *do* mean that!' Hannah told him, with exaggerated sternness. 'And you put me in an awkward position because I'm simply not allowed to talk about it all over the hospital.'

'Sorry. . .' He sighed.

'Are you bored, John? Is that the problem?'

'Yes, that's pretty much it,' he said quickly, and Hannah knew that he had seized on her suggestion as a safe problem to admit to. He probably *was* bored, but that wasn't the only thing that was getting to him.

Kerry Ewbanks appeared in the doorway at that moment. 'Nancy said that you were here, Doctor, but she thought you wouldn't mind if I came in. Hi, John!'

The last two words were added in a tone of shrill

cheerfulness that sounded very insincere to Hannah's
ears.

'I can come back in ten minutes if you'd like to be
alone for a while,' she offered, wondering if it was her
own presence that was inhibiting Kerry.

'No, no, I wouldn't dream of it. You're so busy. You
must have tons of other important stuff to do,' Kerry
gushed unnaturally. 'Please go ahead.'

'All right, then,' Hannah murmured. She glanced at
John's face as she sat down beside him, now gloved,
capped, masked and wearing a fresh gown. His features
were set and wary. 'This shouldn't hurt,' she assured
him, but his expression did not change. 'Please feel
free to talk, Kerry,' she told Mrs Ewbanks. 'But I'll
need you to stay as still as you can, John, and that
means no replies from you, I'm afraid.'

'That's OK,' he growled.

Kerry began a bright, gabbling stream of chatter that
set Hannah's teeth on edge. The flow was punctuated
every few words with a 'darling' or a 'sweetheart,' and
the words didn't sound natural on practical Kerry's
lips.

What on earth was wrong? Hannah wondered. She
was fine when he was in that unresponsive state. She
talked gently, held his hand, showed him just by being
here how much she cared. Now she doesn't want to be
alone with him, doesn't seem to be comfortable about
being here at all. . .

She managed to shut out the distraction of Kerry's
voice at last while she studied John's face. Later this
afternoon she would go over charts, photos, measure-
ments, X-rays, and rehearse the whole procedure in
her mind, but now she needed to take one last look at
damaged muscle, skin and bone in the living patient.
Yes. . . The restructuring she planned to do would be
difficult but not radical, very similar to another patient

she had worked on in London last year. It should all go very well. . .

'Shut up, will you, Kerry!'

Hannah flinched as the man in front of her suddenly stopped being just a series of surgical techniques and became an emotionally complex human being once more. 'Just shut up!' he shouted, then swore graphically and loudly. 'I can't stand this sugar act of yours any more. What the hell has got into you?'

Kerry stepped back, almost pressed against the electronic monitor behind her. She seemed frozen and could not speak. Her husband continued to glower with menace and anger and Hannah instinctively looked at the one figure on the monitor that she could see beyond Kerry's slim frame. His heart-rate had risen significantly. Then suddenly he slumped down and anger drained away.

'It's over,' he said. 'Isn't it? You're not being *you* at all, and what other reason could there be?' He mimicked suddenly, '"What have you done with my wife, you monster? Where's the real Kerry?" You're like something out of a sci-fi movie where the alien takes over a human body. And all I can think is that it means you're not handling this—how I look and how I am and how I'll be, how long it'll take before all this is finally over. You're going to leave me, aren't you? You'll go up to your mother in Sydney with the kids. She'd welcome you with open arms.'

He covered his face with hands that were still bandaged and damaged, and Hannah could see that he was close to tears. She reached out a hand to touch him gently on the shoulder, but before she could make contact, she heard Kerry behind her.

'Don't be a fool, John!' The tone was very brisk and straightforward. 'Honestly! As if I'd leave you over something like this! In fact, you've just lost your last chance to ever get rid of me. Do you really think I'd leave you after I've been through all this fear and torment over whether you'd even *live*? My God, that'd be a poor return on my investment, wouldn't it? And you needn't think you can ever leave *me*, either! All those hours and weeks in here, and then you go off with another woman! Just you ever *try* it, John Ewbanks, and see how far it gets you!'

She was crying and laughing and clinging to any part of him that she could find which wouldn't hurt, and slowly she coaxed a reluctant smile from him and an easing of his tensed shoulders.

'Then why on earth have you been so damned strange, Kerry?'

The petite woman pointed a finger accusingly at Hannah. 'Her fault! She told me to try and show you my love more, and it got me confused, and all self-conscious.'

'I'm sorry, Kerry,' Hannah stammered, appalled at how her well-meant advice had gone wrong. 'I was just concerned that. . .'

'I know you were, Doctor,' Kerry said far too kindly. 'But don't worry. It's all right now, you see. The silly bloke knows now that he's stuck with me for life, thanks to you.'

'Well, I don't see how it was thanks to me,' Hannah answered helplessly.

'Will I be able to kiss this gorgeous woman after the surgery tomorrow?' John came in, squeezing his wife.

'Oh. . .sort of. I doubt you'll want to for a couple of days.'

'Oh, I'll want to!'

'Perhaps I'd better go and. . .' Hannah didn't bother to finish. John and Kerry clearly didn't care *what* she did!

Leaving the ward and travelling down in the lift,

Hannah thought, Well, I suppose that's a happy ending, too, but it doesn't feel like it, from my point of view. It's lucky I never went into psychiatry or social work, if that's how my advice works out!

Arriving at their office in the building across from the main hospital, she asked Annette Kenyon at once, 'Is Eden in yet?'

'With a patient.'

'Oh.'

'He shouldn't be long. And the first one on your list isn't due for another fifteen minutes. Something go wrong in surgery this morning?'

'No. Nothing like that.'

'And everything's OK up in the unit?'

'Fine.'

She could tell that Annette was a bit disappointed. The young receptionist loved to gossip about patients and always seemed to know far more about them than either Eden or Hannah ever had occasion to tell her. They had no reason to believe that she was indiscreet outside of this office. . .but today her attitude irritated Hannah all the same.

I'm not going to tell her about John and Kerry, she decided. No matter how hard she tries to worm something out of me.

But Annette didn't try at all. She must have seen from Hannah's expression that it would be no use. . .

'What's wrong?' said Eden a few minutes later in the blessed sanctuary of his office. He didn't touch her, but there was a kiss in his glance all the same.

'Just tell me I *do* have some sense and some *sensitivity* when it comes to people,' she burst out helplessly, and told him what had happened up in the unit fifteen minutes earlier.

He took her in his arms and cradled her there,

laughing. 'It wasn't in your job description, was it?
Marriage guidance counselling?'

'No, but——'

'Then stop worrying! You were on the right track.
Your intentions were good. You weren't to blame that
Kerry got herself in knots by trying too hard. And they
ended up having a more honest discussion today than
they otherwise might have got around to for weeks.'

'Yes. . .'

'Silly. . . Lovely. . .*very* silly!' He kissed her on the
forehead and on the tip of her nose and, with feathery
lightness for a fraction of a second, on the full lips that
were still pursed in thought. 'Now. . .before Annette
comes in with the coffee I asked for a few minutes
ago. . .'

This time it was a real kiss, soft on her parted lips
and achingly sweet, drawing threads of fire all through
her. When he pulled gently away, it was to say, 'Give
up marriage guidance counselling if you think you have
no talent for it. You're certainly talented enough as a
plastic surgeon and a specialist in burn treatment. And
don't dwell on this. Think about our day together this
weekend instead.'

'Mm-hm, I will. Thanks, Eden.'

Hannah didn't tell him that more than a niggle of
self-doubt on the issue still remained.

CHAPTER NINE

THE noise of the aeroplane droned in the background, threatening to send Hannah off to sleep. For several minutes she resisted, but the page of the fashion magazine in front of her kept blurring in spite of her best efforts, and she doubted that she would do any better this afternoon with the business and current affairs weeklies that Peter Harrison and Alan James were reading in their seats across the aisle.

Next to her Eden was already asleep, and, by pretending that she was craning forward to look out at the landscape of cloud below, Hannah could indulge in watching him. His brow was very smooth and the skin of his eyelids very creamy, though each had a nuance of early summer tan now, as it was nearly the middle of December. Against his cheeks, long lashes formed a dark crescent, and his mouth was curved in the most subtle of smiles, as if his dreams pleased him but he did not want too many people to know it.

It was only just over three months since she was last on a plane, Hannah realised. First coming from London, and then going up to Brisbane to see Gina. If anyone had told her then that she'd be feeling this way about Eden Hartfield. . .!

She closed the magazine and wedged it into the seat pocket in front. Clearly, she wasn't in the mood for reading. Seeing that the two trauma team doctors across the aisle were absorbed in their own magazines, however, she dared to do what she had been wanting to do ever since the plane took off, which was to snuggle down in her seat, close her eyes and let her head nestle into Eden's shoulder.

. . . Feeling this way, and loving every minute of it, her thoughts continued.

He stirred a little and nuzzled against her with his nose, and it was all she could do not to kiss him then and there. The past month had been utterly delightful — a time of discovery, and one of increasing pleasure and certainty in what they felt. Nothing had been said in words about commitment or about the future, but Hannah felt so confident at the moment that she didn't need this. Not yet.

Even the fact that they were keeping the thing fairly secret around the hospital was more of a pleasure than a difficulty. There was no sense that this was clandestine or illicit, and some of those private shared looks between them were delicious.

Together, over the past month, they had explored all the possibilities for filling leisure hours in Canberra: swimming at one of the picnic spots on the Murrumbidgee River; seeing a French film at a highbrow cinema; going to an orchestral concert at the School of Music and a play at the Canberra Theatre Playhouse.

They had eaten memorable meals, too — Indian, Italian, Japanese and French cuisine at restaurants, take-away Lebanese and Vietnamese food atop the look-out on Mount Ainslie or late at night in front of television at his place and barbecues or improvised salads on the tiny patio in the backyard of her own small rented house. Then there were the late, long brunches as they read the Sunday papers, walks in the bush, browsing sessions in art and craft galleries. . .

And last night, too, each with suitcases packed and ready for today's flight, they had sat up until three just talking, not caring that they both had to get up early this morning for rounds and a meeting with Bruce Reith and his temporary sidekick from Sydney.

They had been at Eden's spare yet elegant and comfortable townhouse, and he hadn't wanted her to go home. She hadn't wanted to go, either, but had dragged herself away from his arms and out to her car. It wasn't the first time during the past month that they had played out this scene, but it might be almost the last.

I want to give myself to him so badly, she thought. It might be easier if he was less understanding about it. Then I could hold myself back with anger. But he never pushes, never betrays his frustration, although I know the frustration is there. It's in me, too!

And now they were going away together to Queensland. Five nights with rooms that adjoined along an anonymous convention centre corridor. Was it right? What was she waiting for?

She didn't know, but thought suddenly of Sally. For most women, sex was still what finally bound and cemented a relationship. It contained the seeds of the most bitter betrayal and the most painful loss. Sally might fret during the day over tight finances, a poorly kept-up house, and two boys who missed their father and didn't understand why he was gone, but at night, Hannah felt certain, it was the loneliness of her bed that she sobbed over.

She hadn't seen Sally since that day over a month ago when Eden had struggled so manfully over mowing the lawn. She knew that he went there every weekend now, to help with the garden, and occasionally during the week after work now that it was staying light so late. Sally must be six months pregnant by this time, and heavy work would be even harder for her than it had been before. Presumably she was managing to cope.

But it's the one thing Eden and I never talk about, Hannah realised. Neither of us wants to. We're too afraid. . .

She thought of the conversation she had had over the phone with Gina a few days ago. Before this, she had avoided ringing her sister for several weeks, taking the coward's way out by scribbling a postcard every so often to keep in touch. But, knowing that she would be so close by for the conference, she had wanted to bite the bullet and see Gina, make some real contact.

She felt they hadn't *really* connected since she got back from London. The issue of Steve had always been in the way.

They had arranged to meet on Saturday afternoon, after the last conference session that morning, and before the formal dinner that would wind up the event on Saturday night, and they had promised to try to get together for a quick dinner earlier in the week as well. But the phone conversation had not been a success. Gina's voice had sounded tight and abrupt, as if she was impatient to end the call.

'Sorry, are you in the middle of dinner, or something?' Hannah had asked finally.

'No, it's fine.'

'Is Steve —— ?'

'He's not home yet.'

'Oh, is he working late?' She hoped he was, if it would bring in more money, and if it meant he was taking his life a little more seriously.

'Probably not,' Gina answered shortly. 'Probably at the beach. He's been going there a lot lately.'

'I didn't know he was a surfer.' Hannah kept trying to elicit something more than these terse, ill-tempered replies, but it wasn't working.

'He's not,' Gina said. 'He doesn't even swim, mostly. Just walks. And thinks. He says.'

'Oh. Well, lots of people do that.'

'He's got the car, of course, so I'm stuck here.'

'Yes, that reminds me; on Saturday, do you need—?'

'I'll manage to get down to you. There's a bus, if necessary. Or I may even splurge on a taxi.' She said this last part very defiantly.

Hannah gave up and finished sincerely, 'I'm looking forward to seeing you, Gina. Till then, look after yourself. . .'

'Oh, I definitely will! Don't worry!'

With this cryptic threat, she rang off, leaving Hannah uneasy, and a little angry as well. Whatever was going on, or *not* going on, she had no reason to take it out on her!

Beside her now, Eden stirred, and Hannah realised that she had stiffened as she relived the phone call in her mind. The sleepy contentment she had felt a few minutes earlier had gone, and she was wide awake now. Down the aisle, she heard the clanking of a metal trolley and saw that the flight attendants were bringing tea and coffee, accompanied by a light snack.

Seeing that Peter Harrison and Alan James across the aisle were craning their necks in anticipation, Hannah sat up straight. All four of them had missed meals this morning in their scramble to leave everything in order at the hospital and get to the airport on time. Hannah had managed only Danish pastry and coffee, so this snack, although it was only rolls with cheese, a carrot stick, a piece of fruit and a health-food bar, had her taste buds standing up to attention.

'What's wrong, Hannah?' Eden murmured, his eyes still closed as he tried to snuggle once again into the pillow of soft hair that had been warming his neck.

'They're serving a snack,' she told him, and he awakened fully, too.

He had told her several weeks ago that he would be seeing Steve while at the conference. The news had brought on, she remembered, a familiar moment of tension and dissent over the issue of his brother's relationship with Gina. Since then, it had formed part of the parcel of things they avoided talking about, and she did not know what arrangements he had made. Saturday afternoon was an obvious time. Thursday afternoon was a light one, too, with two sessions scheduled that were only of very minor interest to Eden and Hannah.

I should ask him about it, she thought. It would make sense. For a while it didn't matter that we weren't mentioning Steve and Gina, but now, when we're each going to see them, it's unnatural.

She opened her mouth to speak, while still trying to frame a casual question in her mind and not finding the words. Then, before she could do so, he laughed and pointed out of the window. 'Doesn't that cloud below us look exactly like a hippopotamus on a surfboard?'

Ludicrous, but it did, and Hannah laughed as well, then decided weakly, I won't mention the issue now. Moments later, a snack tray was presented to her and the light meal provided another excuse for letting the subject lapse. Perhaps we'll talk about it tonight. . .she thought half-heartedly.

'Paradoxically, of course, at some of the smaller regional trauma centres in the United States, and I'm sure here as well, staff sometimes find themselves in the situation of *wanting* to see more of a certain type of trauma emergency in order that they can get more experience in how to treat it. That's why we at Robert J. Fitzgerald have instituted an ongoing staff exchange programme with Watts City Hospital in Los Angeles, and so far we've learned. . .'

Hannah couldn't stay to listen to what Dr Myron P. Schultz and his team had learned. She had found the first half of this Wednesday afternoon session interesting, but during the last twenty minutes her attention had begun to flag. The session was going to run late, and she was meeting Gina in the foyer in two minutes.

I wanted to change out of this suit. It'll be hot outside. She'll have to come up to the room with me, she thought.

Gina, however, was a little late. 'The wretched car,' she explained, after squeezing Hannah tightly for a minute. She flicked blonde hair out of her green eyes. 'It kept stalling! I don't know why I'm even surprised any more! Can we go straight off? It's only six but I'm starving for something decent to eat.'

'I want to change first.'

'Oh, why?'

'Because you're in jeans, I'm in a navy blue suit with high heels, and jeans look much more comfortable!'

'Oh, OK, of course, sorry. Sorry I'm grumpy. I need to talk to you so badly, Han. . .'

They went up in the lift to Hannah's room on the fourth floor. The place was quiet at the moment, with most conference delegates still in session, and the empty, carpeted corridor showed off its luxury to maximum effect, uncluttered by people.

'Wow! You specialists sure know how to give yourselves a conference!' Gina said when she saw the spacious, peach-toned room that overlooked the beachfront and the ocean. 'How are you finding the golf courses around here? Up to scratch?'

'Come on, kiddo, you know I don't play golf, and so far I've attended every session. As for cocktail hour tonight, I'm missing that to have dinner with you, so —'

'OK, OK. . .'

Gina wandered restlessly around the room while
Hannah changed. She chose a simple pair of pale khaki
cotton trousers that were pleated at the waist, and
teamed them with a cotton-knit T-shirt in the same
khaki and white. Flat white leather sandals completed
the outfit and. . . Ah! *Much* more comfortable. It only
took five minutes to make the change.

'Where do you want to go?' she asked as they waited
for lifts, which were much busier now. The session
must have ended.

'Oh, anywhere. Not pizza. I'm heartily sick of the
stuff. The restaurant here?' Gina finished hopefully.

'Not dressed like that, love.'

'Oh. Yes, I should have thought to. . .' She looked
down at the jeans and very pretty but very casual pink
top that accompanied them. 'I really had a yen for
lobster, too. . .'

The lift gave a ping that signalled its imminent
arrival, and at that moment Hannah saw Eden breast-
ing the staircase at the far end of the corridor. He had
obviously grown impatient with the wait in the lift-bay
on the ground floor. Intensely aware of him even at
this distance, she prayed that he wouldn't see her, or
Gina, and cursed the long seconds that the lift doors
seemed to be taking before they opened. At last they
did so and the two women entered. Hannah reached
immediately for the 'Door Close' button and let out a
sigh of relief as Eden's figure, coming ever closer along
the corridor towards them now, finally disappeared
from view.

Gina had seen him, though. 'Are you seeing much
of Eden these days?' she asked, as the lift made its
smooth descent.

'Well, we see each other a lot at work, of course,'
Hannah hedged.

'But no more picnics? Good! I'm glad to hear it!'

Gina answered her own question without leaving time for Hannah to give a response. She could have corrected the assumption, of course, but. . . No decent excuse for it, she just *didn't*.

Ten minutes of exploring around the vicinity of the convention centre brought them to a pleasant-looking restaurant, decorated in coral and sea-tones, that served mainly light, imaginative pastas and salads, and soon they had sat down in a corner by the window and ordered their meal.

'You said you wanted to talk,' Hannah prompted gently when brimming glasses of chilled white wine arrived.

Gina sighed. 'Do you really want to hear?'

'Of course!'

'Bleah! Things are just a mess, that's all. He won't make any decisions. At least, we don't make any decisions *together*. I ask about a job and he just shrugs and tells me to do what I want. He tells me when it's already a *fait accompli* that he *won't* be joining this group practice permanently as we'd talked about and been hoping for all along.'

'Do you know if —— ?'

But Gina swept on and Hannah kept silent after this. 'Then I find letters from a couple of hospitals down south and he admits he's been sounding out possibilities in Sydney and Melbourne. He stays late at work and I *know* he's been using the phone there to ring Sally in private, because the practice bills its staff for personal long-distance calls and last week he had to write them an *enormous* cheque to cover his share. Hannah, I don't know what's happening, and I don't know what to do. You're ten years older than me, and you must have had some experience with men, though you've never told me much about it. For a start, why aren't *you* married? You're bloody gorgeous, successful, and—but that's beside the point. I want some guidance, some counselling! Should I leave him? Make him *talk* properly? Get him to promise to start the paperwork for a divorce? *Tell* me!'

'*Tell* you? Just like that?'

'Yes, damn it!'

'How can I, Gina?' she queried helplessly.

Heaped and steaming plates of pasta had arrived, but both women only toyed at them with limp forks. Hannah thought about John and Kerry Ewbanks and how her well-meant advice there had gone wrong a month ago, creating days of unnecessary and unspoken tension before each had exploded in anger and come to understand what was wrong.

She still felt badly about that, when she thought of how easily they might have missed the necessary confrontation and dug themselves deeper and deeper into misunderstanding. And they had a very strong relationship to start with! Gina's and Steve's, on the other hand, had seemed anything *but* strong from the beginning.

'*Haven't* you had any sort of experience that might help?' Gina was saying in a demanding, desperate tone. 'Don't you even have an opinion?'

'Time for the story of Patrick, I guess,' Hannah said flippantly.

'The story of Patrick?'

'Yes. . .' She told it, and it took a long time.

'Whew!' Gina whistled at the end of it, clearly looking at her older sister with new eyes. 'Four years! A torrid, illicit affair!'

'Please don't invest it with any glamour, Gina. It didn't have any.'

'You're telling me! It sounds like hell from start to finish.'

Hannah didn't know whether to feel pleased at this

strong response or not. She had deliberately tried to make those years sound as miserable and doomed as possible, but now she wondered whether that was fair.

I *do* want her to leave Steve, Hannah realised. But I'm not prepared to say so straight out. I'm not laying my cards on the table at all.

She came in quickly aloud, 'But that's *my* story, not yours. In the end, I *can't* tell you what to do. I *won't*! Only you can decide. Or you and Steve.'

'Me and Steve?' Gina echoed cynically. 'I just told you, we never decide anything. It just goes on from day to day.'

She bent over her pasta in gloomy silence and began to shovel it in, her hunger clearly a symptom of inner turmoil as she didn't give herself time to actually enjoy the food.

She's put on weight, Hannah noticed belatedly. So far it suits her. She isn't quite so wraith-like. But a few more kilos and she'll start to look pudgy, which won't suit her at all! I guess if she's not working and isn't particularly happy, she just drifts around their flat all day and munches . . .

With a reduced appetite, she turned to her own meal.

'We keep missing each other,' said a familiar voice behind Hannah two evenings later as she waited for the lift to go up to her room.

It was Eden, and she turned to him, hiding some of her pleasure at seeing him. . .but not all of it. He was looking down at her, his blue eyes warm and almost as caressing as his touch.

'Our sessions keep finishing at slightly different times,' she answered him.

In order to cover everything that was of relevance to their own particular interests, they had worked out in advance which of them was to go to which seminar, as almost every session was in conflict with something of equal importance. It was a big conference.

'And when we *do* meet,' he went on, 'like at lunchtime today, there are usually rather too many other people around for my taste. I looked for you on Wednesday evening, but I couldn't find you.'

Remembering how she had hidden from him in the lift because of Gina's presence, Hannah capped his accusation hastily. 'And *I* looked for *you* on Thursday.'

'Hmm.' His eyes narrowed slightly. 'Then I guess we've both been catching up on family business.'

Peter Harrison joined them at that moment, enthusiastic about the seminar he had been to this afternoon, and then came a crowd of orthopaedic surgeons, each as burly as the stereotype dictated. Their arrival coincided with that of the lift, and one of them cornered Eden with exclamations of surprise and pleasure as they entered it.

'Eden! I didn't realise you'd be at this do. I only arrived this morning, myself. Good to see you after so long! Where are you these days?'

Eden's enthusiasm was more restrained but equally genuine, and they spent the stop-start lift ride to the fourth floor trying to arrange a time to get together. 'Not tonight, I'm afraid, Ron. I have dinner plans already.'

His questioning glance sought and met Hannah's eyes, and she understood his meaning and gave a quick, happy nod.

'Well, we'll just have to meet up at the formal dinner tomorrow,' was the orthopaedist's conclusion a minute later. Hannah, thinking about tonight, hadn't heard the intervening discussion.

The lift arrived at the fourth floor and she and Eden got out, along with several other people, including

Peter Harrison, whose room adjoined Eden's on the far side.

'Knock on your door in an hour?' the latter said in an undertone, as Hannah stopped at her door and produced the key.

'Lovely!' she replied, and a moment later she was alone.

It was a delightful interlude. So far, for those who had *not* taken time off for golf or water-sports, the conference schedule had been hectic, and in her few spare minutes Hannah had spent much time mulling over Gina's problems and her own potential for solving them. Now, with Eden's company to look forward to this evening, she did not think about Steve and Gina at all.

Instead, she spent the time relaxing in a bath, blow-drying her full halo of dark hair into a shaping of light yet sophisticated waves, and putting on her dark crimson silk dress with toning make-up and matching shoes and jewellery. Then, still with ten minutes to spare, she sat out on the cool, shady balcony that overlooked the beach and watched the last of the surfers, who were taking advantage of a recent storm out at sea and catching some impressive waves. . .

'Hey! You're not answering your door!' Eden called accusingly from the neighbouring balcony.

'Oh, my goodness!' She looked across at him and scrambled to her feet guiltily, then could only blurt the truth. 'I was in such a dreamy state of anticipation about seeing you that I forgot it was actually time to come and let you in!'

He laughed and they both came over to the wide railing of the balcony to stand there for several giddy, foolish minutes simply gazing at each other. The balconies were about eight feet apart, and they could not touch, but for some reason neither of them seemed to want the moment to end. An evening breeze teased at his dark hair, and he looked immaculate in his charcoal-grey suit with that perfectly white shirt beneath.

'Nutty woman!' he said at last in a caressing tone.

'Crazy man!' she returned very softly.

Their meal was perfect. He had used the previous hour more productively than she had, wangling a booking at one of the area's top restaurants, high above the beach and the water. Since they had arrived at just after seven, they had plenty of time to linger over each course, and they did so, consulting a sommelier about wine, refreshing their palates with tangy grapefruit sorbet between courses, and sampling a cheese platter as well as dessert. It took nearly three hours; they talked, he even kissed her across the table after moving the long, tapering candles aside, and both of them knew as they left the restaurant that the evening was not yet over.

Hannah's heart began to pound as they reached her door. She knew what she was going to say, and knew that she wanted it, but that didn't mean she was not afraid.

'Are you coming in?' It came out so low that he must barely have heard.

'Am I invited?'

'Yes, you are, Eden.' Both of them knew that it was not just an invitation to her room, but to her bed.

Her hand trembled slightly as she took out her key, and he saw this, pulled it gently from her fingers and inserted it in the lock himself. When the door had opened, he held her by the hand and drew her inside as if this was his room and he had been the one to issue the invitation. It was a tender touch of mastery that she was deeply grateful for, and everything that followed beneath them contained this same nuance of gentleness, tenderness, and respect.

When she touched a light-switch and found that the room was suddenly flooded with far too harsh a light, he switched it off again and turned a table-lamp in the far corner of the room to its dimmest setting, leaving the two of them in a soft golden glow that was just right. And when her fingers fumbled at the buttons of her dress, which fastened asymmetrically to one side, he took over the task, then slipped the dress off her shoulders with a caressing touch so that it fell to the floor at her feet.

He gasped at the full swelling of her breasts that threatened, with her quickened breathing, to spill from the lacy black cups of her bra, but did not let himself hurry even the smallest movement as he slipped the fastening undone then moved to the elastic waist of her matching briefs. In the warm air, her nakedness before him was incredibly sensual and utterly safe, and when he stood before her, moments later, stripped of his own clothing, their coming together brought both of them immediately to a shuddering pitch of urgency.

It all felt so right, and it lasted a long time. When they finally lay together, fully spent, in the darkness, sensuality slipped effortlessly into sleepiness and he cradled her beneath the sheets until she drifted away. She hadn't intended to sleep so soon. She had wanted to lie there simply enjoying him, dreaming over him, feeling the warmth and weight of the hands that cupped her breasts then moved lazily to her hips and thighs. . . But somehow sleep came all on its own, and so soundly that she did not stir all night.

When she did awaken, tangled languorously in the sheets, the bed felt immediately colder and she realised at once that Eden was gone.

I didn't notice, and I suppose he didn't want to wake me. . .she told herself.

The windows were thickly curtained, but the strong

light seeping in at their edges told her that she must have slept in. The last working session on the conference began at nine this morning, and it was one that they had both planned to attend. Eden had woken in time, it seemed, but. . .

'I'll have to skip breakfast,' she realised.

A knock sounded at her door at that moment, and she knew it must be him, coming to prompt her into rising. Hastily, she slipped her arms into a blue silk kimono, pulling it across the front of her body and feeling his caressing hands again in the guise of the silk's cool touch.

She pulled open the front door. 'Hi, I'm awake. Sorry, is it — ?'

But it wasn't Eden Hartfield who stood there at all; it was Gina.

CHAPTER TEN

'No, I'M not the chambermaid,' Gina said. 'Thank God you're here! Otherwise, I'd have had to come and round you up out of your seminar. Let me in, and help me with that suitcase. It's nearly killed me all the way from the bus.'

'What on earth ——?'

'Isn't it obvious? I've left him. Oh, God!' She suddenly burst into tears and fled into Hannah's arms, her much smaller frame in startling contrast to Eden's body that had so recently been there. 'It's over!' Gina sobbed. 'And I've been such a fool!'

She took a long time to calm down, and said little that was coherent. When Hannah had finally soothed her, she said, 'I'll make you some tea, shall I? And we'll talk about this properly.'

'I'd love some,' Gina sniffed. She began to talk again as Hannah went to a bench-top in the corner of the luxurious peach-toned room, where tea and coffee-making facilities were set up above a tiny fridge. 'He's going to go back to Sally. Can you believe that?'

'How do you know?' Hannah asked as neutrally as she could. The news affected her in so many ways that she didn't know what to feel. . .didn't even know whether or not to believe the melodramatic announcement.

'Eden was there all Thursday afternoon and he stayed the night. This is all his fault. . . No, it's not. But I know it was all they talked about. Steve didn't come to bed till almost three on Thursday night.'

She began to pace the room restlessly as she talked.

Hannah was walking too, but with more purpose. One of the cups she needed for the tea was on the night-table beside the bed. And as she picked it up, she saw the scrawled note from Eden.

Hannah, didn't want to wake you, you looked so ——

Before she could read further, she became aware that Gina was staring in accusation.

'Just a note about yesterday's session. I don't need it any more.' She crumpled it up and tossed it into the bin beneath the table, not knowing what else she could do. She would retrieve it later, of course. Gina still glowered. 'I *was* listening, Gee. . .' Hannah faltered.

'So what was the last thing I said?'

'Oh, that you. . .that you. . .'

'I *eavesdropped*, Hannah. I couldn't sleep. It must have been at about two, and I crept out into the corridor to where I could hear. Eden was saying it to Steve straight out. "I've talked to Sally and I know she'll take you back if things have really changed, if you've really learned something from this torrid little episode. You don't really care about this girl, do you? She's just a symptom. Sally's prepared to understand that." Blah, blah; he went on some more, but. . .'

'A *symptom*?'

'Yes!' She gave a high, hard laugh. 'The rest of it I'm paraphrasing, of course, but that was the exact word. I'm a symptom, Hannah. God, I hate that man!'

'Steve?'

'Eden! Self-righteous, supercilious, egotistical, puritanical. . .'

Could this be *her* Eden? Hannah wondered help-lessly. And *was* he her Eden? She felt a desperate need to see him as soon as possible.

Then she saw Gina sink on to the bed and begin to

sob again. 'And do you know the worst thing about the bloody man?'

'Eden?'

'Yes, Eden! Of course Eden! It's that he's *right*! All along that's all I've been. A symptom of the fact that Steve didn't know what he wanted out of life.'

The electric jug boiled and Hannah made the tea, finding some plain, sweet biscuits to go with each cup and saucer. Probably this was all the breakfast she would get. A surreptitious look at the watch on the bedside table had told her that it was already after ten.

They talked for a long time. While they were each draining a second cup of tea, the chambermaid arrived to do the room, so Hannah dressed quickly and they sat on the balcony, where Gina's hair caught the morning light, her tears dried, and she began to look a little better.

'So what are you going to do, love?' Hannah said to her at last.

'Stay here tonight and fly back to Canberra with you tomorrow, if I can. I've brought all my stuff — all that I want, that is. I left a note for Steve. Quite a *long* note! So I've burnt my boats. And I'm glad! I've been such a fool, Han! The whole reason I was attracted to him in the first place was that he was so *domestic*. No, there were other things, too — his sense of humour, his quirky, impulsive ideas. His looks, of course. But basically, that's what I want, Hannah — a house and kids. So I pick a man who only wants me because he's having a temporary mid-life crisis and wants to escape from that! Intelligent move on my part, wasn't it?'

'Don't make yourself feel worse by thinking that way,' Hannah said gently. 'Sometimes the best lessons we learn about ourselves are the ones that come the hardest.'

'Tell me that again in six months!'

'Will you go back to work at the health centre?'

'No. Even if Steve doesn't go back there himself, I need a change. I'm going to travel. Maybe for quite a long time. A couple of years. Nurses can get work overseas. I need to get this out of my system. Then, when I'm ready, I'll come back and find myself the right kind of man. . .and I'll turn into a Sally Hartfield myself, the picture of domestic bliss. I *want* that, Hannah! Isn't it crazy?'

'I thought you hated Sally.'

'Oh, I don't really. I've never even met her. Used to take messages from her for Steve when she rang the health centre. She's probably a terrific person.'

She is. . .especially if she'll take Steve back after all this, Hannah wanted to say, but wisely restrained herself.

'So. . .mind if we share that house for a while, till I've made my travel plans and done enough agency work to get some money together?'

'It sounds nice.'

'Now, can we go and get some lunch and spend the afternoon on the beach?'

It *was* lunchtime already. In fact, it was exactly the hour when the last conference session was due to finish. Delegates would not foregather again until tonight's formal dinner at seven. Hannah had been planning all along to spend the afternoon with Gina, but now she found herself wondering frantically about Eden, and how he was spending the rest of the day.

'Supercilious, puritanical. . .' and fresh from her bed. She felt churned up, confused, and remembered too late, as she came in from the balcony with Gina, that the chambermaid would have emptied out the contents of the waste-paper bins, including that unread note Eden had left her.

'Let's just grab a salad roll and some juice somewhere and go straight to the beach,' Gina suggested.

It didn't take them long to get ready, and, with a
smartly cut black and turquoise bathing suit beneath
her baggy cotton shorts and blouse now, Hannah was
eager to leave the room. Last night it had been such a
private, passionate haven. Now it felt claustrophobic
and close.

She opened the door, Gina followed her. . .and they
both almost cannoned into Steve and Eden who were
just about to enter the latter's room next door. For a
long moment, all four of them were frozen into silence.
Steve was dressed casually in jeans, with a plaid cotton
shirt stretched across his broad shoulders. He carried a
beach towel and a plastic shopping bag containing
swimming-costume, block-out cream and other
supplies.

Eden was more formally dressed in dark tailored
trousers and one of his trademark pale blue shirts that
did something quite magic to the colour of his eyes. He
had obviously met up with Steve by arrangement
straight after the morning conference session.

Steve made a strangled sound deep in his throat.
Gina gave a tiny, horrified cry. Hannah couldn't think
or say anything at all. That only left Eden, and,
typically, he was the first to recover some degree of
control.

'We've rented the boat from one o'clock onwards,
Steve, so let's get going,' he said as he opened the door
of his room. His eyes did not meet Hannah's at all. A
second later, he and Steve had both disappeared.

The banquet-room was noise-filled and brightly lit.
Conversation drummed and swelled, occasionally
punctuated by bursts of laughter from different tables.
Glints and glows bounced off chandeliers and wine

glasses, and the white tablecloth seemed as harsh as fluorescent lighting.

I have a headache, Hannah realised belatedly. I was too long in the sun this afternoon.

She also had a lump in her throat.

'The chicken or the rack of lamb, madam?' said a waiter behind her shoulder.

'Oh. . .the lamb,' she answered, not caring and not feeling hungry. 'And a glass of water as well, please.'

Toying with the food in front of her, Hannah knew she was putting a dampener on the conversation at this end of the table of twelve. There were only two other women here, down the far end, and several of the men at this end had looked pleased at first that this glamorous-looking plastic surgeon had chosen their table, and their end of it. They didn't know that she had sat down quite absently, not caring about the matter at all.

She *was* glamorous tonight, though. The dress had been packed five days ago back in Canberra — with Eden in mind, of course. Tonight, if there had been any other choice, she would have taken it. It was a black cocktail-length fall of silk with narrow straps, a rather low back and a curved neckline that showed off, just a little, the full symmetry of her breasts. With high-heels, and matching earrings and necklace in black and silver, she *looked* tall, slim and very elegant. . . and *felt* uncomfortable, out of place and miserable.

Having committed herself to this table half an hour ago, she had realised too late that it gave her a perfect line of sight across the room to where Eden sat with his back to her. He had Steve beside him. One of the other delegates must have cancelled attendance at this last event, and Eden had taken advantage of the informal seating arrangements to get permission for his brother to join him.

The orthopaedic surgeon from the lift yesterday,

Ron, was with them, too. The three formed an ani-
mated group, in contrast to the glum corner of her own
table, and she realised that she simply had to pull
herself out of this mood, not just for the sake of her
table companions, but for her own self-esteem as well.

'Have you travelled far for this conference?' Turning
with a bright expression to the man on her left, she
resolutely attacked her lamb at the same time.

The meal, complete with after-dinner speaker, was
over at last. 'Would you like to join me in the bar?'
said Hannah's table companion, who had turned out to
be a likeable enough surgeon from New Zealand.

'Actually, I'm rather tired and I have my sister here
tonight,' she told him.

It was only the truth. Her feet ached in the high
shoes and the neckline of her dress chafed at her
breasts where last night Eden's fingers had been so
tender and so magically sensual. And Gina had been
alone in the room all evening, refusing to consider a
meal by herself in the hotel's second, less-formal
restaurant. 'I'll order room-service,' she had said.

The New Zealander offered to escort Hannah
upstairs, but she said no to this as well. She didn't want
to have to ask him in for coffee, or make an excuse for
not asking him in if he seemed to expect it, and she
was worried about Gina. In spite of the younger
woman's resolutions about travel and a fresh start, she
was very down in the dumps. . .and who could blame
her?

She was down in the dumps herself, Hannah realised.

On the beach that afternoon, returning to the room
at five, and leaving it again two hours later to go down
to dinner she had been terrified each time that they
would encounter Steve with Eden, and that some
terrible scene would erupt. They hadn't seen the two
men, however, and Eden had made no attempt to see

Hannah alone. No note slipped under the door. No phone call. And she didn't dare to leave a message for him.

It was an impossible situation: to have slept with a man for the first time. . .to ache with a love for him that she had not yet dared to speak of to anyone. . . and to be unable to see him, talk to him, because her sister and his brother had just ended a difficult, doomed and unsanctioned affair and were now camping in adjoining hotel rooms.

At least, Gina was camping. Steve, presumably, would drive back to the flat later tonight in that crummy old car.

'I don't care what he does with the flat *or* the car,' Gina had said earlier today. 'I don't feel that I owe him any money, and if he sells the car and gets the bond money back from the flat when he gives up the lease, then he's welcome to keep the proceeds. I just want a clean break.'

She had managed to book a seat on Hannah's flight tomorrow, and the two of them would be checking out of here first thing.

I hope she *has* been all right, Hannah thought as she slipped through the crowds of diners who were milling about now, making arrangements for the rest of the evening. Perhaps I should have cancelled the dinner, and refused to leave her alone. . .

But she had wanted so badly to see Eden without Gina around, even though she was afraid of their encounter at the same time. Somehow, she had been assuming that if she went to the dinner she would bump into him, he would be alone, too; they would touch and talk, and. . .

'Oops, sorry, Hannah.' It *was* Eden, crossing her path just as she was about to reach the main door.

'Oh, Eden. . .' She was flushed and awkward

immediately as she looked up at him. He was immaculately dressed, of course, in a black evening suit and crisp white shirt. On the dance-floor, where many people were now heading, they would have made a stunning couple. Would he ask her to dance, and at last, in the crowd, would they find some time to make real contact again, to rediscover what they had had together last night. . .?'

Steve was still with him. She saw this belatedly as Eden stepped aside a little. 'You know my brother, don't you?' The blandest of lines, but she sensed an undercurrent of wariness — was it wariness? — that she didn't understand.

All he has to do is squeeze my hand, look at me, touch me, and I'll know it's all right, she thought.

But he didn't do any of these things. 'Steve? You remember Hannah?' Still very netural, very controlled.

'Yes. Yes. Nice to see you again.'

It was awkward of course, and Hannah could easily have made it more so by pointing out to Steve that Gina was probably sobbing her heart out over him right at this moment up on the fourth floor. She didn't, of course, because all she wanted to do was to get away. The two men clearly felt the same.

'Well, Steve, we were going to. . .'

'Yes. Yes,' Steve agreed hastily.

'I'm. . .very sorry that we couldn't sit together this evening,' Eden said to Hannah, and at last he allowed his eyes to meet hers. But she looked quickly away. Sorry, was he? How pointless to say such a thing! What had stopped him from sitting with her? He didn't have to invite Steve tonight, if that was all it was.

'Yes, some other time, perhaps.' She murmured the meaningless conventional phrase then added a quick, 'Goodnight.' A gap had opened in the crowd of people and she took advantage of it to slip quickly through before it closed again, all her pulses pounding and her head feeling like a drum. Just last night, would she have believed that she could be this miserable today?

When Hannah reached the room on the fourth floor, she found that her fears of anything dramatic having happened in her absence were unfounded. Gina was slumped in front of television, using a remote control to flick back and forth between channels. She was snacking on sweet biscuits and said that she had enjoyed the hamburger that she had had sent up.

'And. . .how are you?'

'You mean in my innermost self?' came the dry question. 'Oh. . .rotten, of course. Laugh about it sometimes. Don't worry about me, Han. I'm going to be fine. It'll just take time.'

Neither slept well, of course. Hearing Hannah return from a pointless trip to the bathroom to splash her face, Gina croaked wearily out of the darkness, '*You* shouldn't be tossing and turning, Han, just because *I'm* unhappy!' and Hannah didn't dare to confess that right at this moment it was her own miserable uncertainty over Eden, and her almost feverish memories of last night that were keeping her from sleep.

Morning came at last, and then the ride by courtesy bus to the airport some distance away. Hannah didn't even know if Eden would be on this flight. Somehow, it hadn't seemed important to ask earlier in the week. Now, of course, she longed to know whether it was fruitless to be looking at every dark head, every masculine silhouette that she saw, and whether it was a waste of energy to be wondering what she would say to him, or if she would manage to say anything at all with Gina glowering beside her.

'The check-in is crowded,' Gina said. 'I suppose Christmas and the school holidays are almost upon us.

I was lucky to get a flight. It would have been unendur-
able, having to stay.'

'You could have gone by bus,' Hannah said absently.
Was that him ahead in the line? No. . .

Minutes passed and they approached the head of the
queue, which now snaked behind them as well. The
number of newcomers was dwindling, though. It was
almost time to board. He wasn't coming. Hannah
didn't know whether to be glad or sorry.

'Got your ticket, Han? And are you keeping this bag
for cabin luggage?' Gina prompted. They had reached
the check-in counter.

'Oh, yes, but this suitcase is going with the cargo.'
She hefted it on to the scales.

'No, it's not.' Eden Hartfield's hand pulled it away
just as the check-in clerk was about to haul it on to the
conveyor belt that would take it away.

Both women turned to him, Hannah with a gasp and
Gina with a hiss.

'If you've come to tell me——' the latter began, but
Eden interrupted impatiently.

'This has nothing to do with you, Gina,' he said. He
looked scruffy this morning, in contrast to his perfect
tailoring last night. His hair was tousled as if he had
forgotten to brush it, a blue and white striped cotton
shirt dangled part of its tail over the back pocket of his
jeans, and his face looked creased and tight. Somehow,
this unlikely combination of attributes made him
utterly gorgeous. 'Get your boarding pass and put your
luggage through.'

'But——' Gina bleated.

'It's Hannah I'm here for.' He turned to her, took
her shoulders in hands that chafed them urgently and
spoke in a low, intense tone. 'I can't accept what
happened yesterday. I've been awake all night thinking
about it. I was going to accept it, just let you take this

flight and then pick up again at work as if we were two cordial colleagues who barely knew each other's first names, but. . . I can't believe you've taken this way of telling me that the past month. . .and Friday night. . . meant nothing. You didn't even answer my note!'

'I didn't know it needed an answer.'

'Didn't *know*. . .?'

'I didn't get a chance to read it.'

'But I left it ——'

'We can't talk now, Eden,' she implored him, her heart pounding and her skin alive to his demanding touch beneath the Wedgwood-blue jersey-knit dress she wore.

'We're *going* to talk now!' he hissed.

'Gina. . .'

'Gina is taking this flight. *You* are not. You have the keys to the house, don't you?' he said, turning to the younger woman.

'My neighbour has them, but ——'

'She can't go alone, Eden.'

'She's an adult, isn't she?'

'Yes, but ——'

'I'll "but" you if I hear that word one more time! Damn it, woman!' He pulled her roughly and impatiently into his arms and began to kiss her with a domination he had not shown before. The many onlookers were enthralled, of course, and Gina gaped like a fish. 'Have I really got this all wrong? Is it an issue of loyalty to your sister, or ——?'

'Not here, Eden. . .'

'Then you'd better come with me, hadn't you? Because I'm going to kiss you and I'm going to get some answers from you whether it's here or in the middle of the convention centre foyer or on live television. The past twenty-four hours have been hell and I'm not putting up with the torture a moment longer!'

'Gina. . .?' Hannah, with fiery flushes coming and going all over her, fought free of Eden — although somehow one arm stayed caressingly around his waist — and turned to her younger sister. 'Is it all right . . .if you do go back alone? Eden's right. We have things to discuss. I'll take a later flight today — '

'Or tomorrow. Or the next day,' Eden came in with a growl.

'There's a lot you haven't been telling me, isn't there?' Gina said, her teeth clenched ominously.

'I. . .yes. . . I. . .'

The two sisters looked at each other for a long moment, grey eyes rather beseeching, green eyes with a distinct glitter. Then Gina suddenly relaxed and gave a helpless shrug. 'Well, all I can say is. . .at least he's not married!'

She tucked in the corner of her mouth and rolled her eyes, then suddenly she was laughing and hugging Hannah, whispering in her ear, 'If he's right for you, go for it! I'll have to revise my previous opinion, but. . . I'm doing a lot of that at the moment, and I think it's good for me!' Releasing her sister, she added, 'Now, let me get on this flight, or it'll leave without me, not to mention these other people behind, and they'll all curse me forever.' She picked up her ticket and boarding pass and left the queue. 'Don't wait to see me off, you two.'

'We won't,' growled Eden, raking a hand impatiently through those untidy waves of dark hair.

But Hannah gave Gina another hard squeeze, and both sisters had tears in their eyes as they said goodbye.

'At last,' was Eden's comment as he took Hannah's suitcase and began to stride away.

'Where are we going?' she asked in a small voice.

He stopped abruptly and dumped the suitcase on to the floor. 'Good question. I have a rented car out in the car park, but I'm damned if I'm going to wait until we get into that and drive it somewhere romantic before I thrash this out with you. In which case. . .why not here?'

'Here?'

'Yes.' He faced her, and both were immediately oblivious to the traffic of people moving up and down the concourse in search of check-in counters and departure gates. 'Hannah, why didn't you read my note? My very, very important note.'

'Because Gina had arrived before I found it, and she was so angry with you. . . I pretended it was garbage and threw it away, and the chambermaid got to it before I could get it back again.' It all sounded stupid now, alone with him again, but yesterday morning Gina's feelings had been very dominant in the hotel room. 'What. . .what did it say, Eden?'

'Well, it's going to sound foolish like this.'

'Not, it won't,' she told him firmly.

'No? All right, then.' His voice dropped suddenly to a caressing pitch and he bent very closely over her as he spoke. 'Well, the note began by explaining that you looked so lovely asleep that the writer of the note could not bear to wake you. Then it went on to ask what you thought of a medical conference dinner as the setting for a proposal of marriage.'

'Oh!' came a tiny cry from Hannah.

'It further suggested. . .that if you thought the setting appropriate, you might let the writer know during the morning session, so that the two of you could arrange to sit together that night. It explained that the writer was meeting his brother immediately after the session ended, and that to wait any longer for your answer would be torture... And torture it was, Hannah. Can't you put me out of my misery now?'

'A conference dinner is a lovely setting for a proposal of marriage, Eden,' she whispered happily, pillowing her head against his chest and brushing away two tears of relief and love and a hundred other feelings. 'But I can think of a better one.'

'You can?'

'How about the middle of an airport on a busy Sunday morning?'

'I see your point. We may not be going to any more conference dinners in the near future.'

'Exactly. We're both a little impatient about this, aren't we?'

'We are. So, Hannah, could you please, please marry me very soon?'

'Do you want a big wedding?' he asked much later as they lay together on the grass in the shade at the lushly tropical botanical gardens near Mount Coot-tha.

It was serendipity that had brought them to this spot, as each had been in too much of a happy daze to consult a map or make a decision about routes and destinations. They had no picnic rug to lie on, of course, and the grass was quite tickly on Hannah's bare arms and legs, but somehow that didn't seem to matter.

'A big wedding? You mean with a band and a hundred and fifty guests in a big catering hall?'

'That sort of thing.'

She made a face, and he kissed the crease that had suddenly appeared between her arched brows. 'It doesn't appeal,' she admitted.

'Good.'

'I like your emphatic tone. What would have happened if I'd said two hundred and fifty guests, please, and a fleet of stretch limousines for the twelve bridesmaids?'

'I'm thinking of Sally and Steve, love,' he answered her, his blue eyes very serious all at once.

'Then Gina was right. She said you had persuaded Steve to — '

'I didn't persuade him to do anything. She has no reason to be angry with me, and I think she'll see that eventually. I helped Steve to make some decisions he should have made long ago. And, yes, they're going to try and give their marriage another chance.'

'It isn't going to be easy, after all that's happened.'

'It's going to be by far the hardest thing he's ever done, and a huge challenge for Sally as well. She has a lot to forgive. Are you sorry it's happening?'

'Of course not. Eden, honestly! What do you think? That — ' He kissed her into silence.

'I think we both feel the same about the whole thing now, don't we?'

'I think perhaps we always did. We both hated being caught in the middle, and we just wanted everyone to have — '

'The kind of happiness that we'll have,' he agreed, nuzzling her neck. 'But it wouldn't help anyone if Gina and Sally bumped into each other while dancing at our wedding, would it?'

'Don't worry. Gina is going to travel overseas for a couple of years, do some nursing work in America, or in Africa with Australian Volunteers Abroad. I think it's a good plan.'

'And Steve is going to specialise in orthopaedics, at long last.'

'Whew!'

'He should have done it five years ago. He's finally realised that what he needs is a mental challenge, not an easy group practice in which to coast along for the sake of funding a mortgage he can barely manage to pay.'

'Then. . .'

'Yes, they'll be selling the house and moving to Sydney, where they'll have to rent something much smaller. Sally won't mind a bit, I don't think, as long as Steve is happy. And with a demanding speciality to get his teeth into, I know he will be. Ron Gibson, who I met up with on Friday in the lift, is going to cut some red tape on his behalf and take him on at South Sydney Hospital.'

'Then for a while, at least, it'll be just us left in Canberra,' Hannah said thoughtfully.

'Are you sorry?'

'At the moment? Not a bit! I think we've earned some time where we're *not* in the middle of the rest of the family's problems. Some time to ourselves.'

'Time to ourselves. . .' he echoed caressingly. 'That's just how I hope our wedding will be, since it can't be a family affair. Down at the coast, perhaps, where I have the beach house.'

'*On* the beach?'

'On the beach. . .with just the two of us.'

'Eden, I think we need someone to perform the ceremony, don't we?'

'And someone to witness it. But somehow I think we'll scarcely notice them.'

'I think you're probably right. . .'

Perhaps they were just an unobservant couple. At any rate, when he kissed her again, his whole body warm against hers even in the cool of the shade, neither of them noticed the group of seagulls parading to and fro across the lawn all around them in search of food, nor the families enjoying a Sunday outing, nor even the sudden noise of an aeroplane overhead. It could have been Gina's plane on its way to Canberra. It probably wasn't.

'Nothing matters in the world to me today except us,' Eden whispered against Hannah's mouth. 'And I think it's going to be that way for a long time. . .'

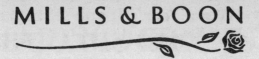

Win a Year's Supply of romances
ABSOLUTELY FREE!

YES! you could win a whole year's supply of Mills & Boon romances by playing the Treasure Trail Game. Its simple! - there are seven separate items of treasure hidden on the island, follow the instructions for each and when you arrive at the final square, work out their grid positions, (i.e **D4**) and fill in the grid reference boxes.

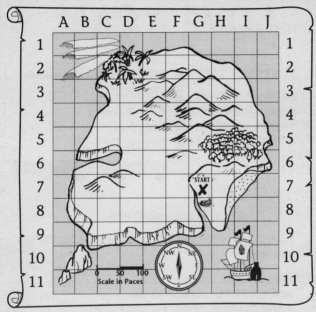

From the start, walk 250 paces to the **North**.

GRID REFERENCE

From this position walk 150 paces **South**.

GRID REFERENCE

Then 100 **South**.

GRID REFERENCE

Now turn **West** and walk 150 paces.

GRID REFERENCE

Now take 100 paces **East**.

GRID REFERENCE

And finally 50 paces **East**.

GRID REFERENCE

Please turn over for entry details

SEND YOUR ENTRY
NOW!

The first five correct entries picked out of the bag after the closing date will each win one year's supply of Mills & Boon romances (six books every month for twelve months - worth over £90). What could be easier?

Don't forget to enter your name and address in the space below then put this page in an envelope and post it today (you don't need a stamp).

Competition closes 28th Feb '95.

TREASURE TRAIL Competition
FREEPOST
P.O. Box 236
Croydon
Surrey CR9 9EL

Are you a Reader Service subscriber?   Yes ☐   No ☐

Ms/Mrs/Miss/Mr _____ COMTT

Address _____

_____

_____

_____ Postcode _____

Signature _____